The Case of the Kona Curse

by

Emily Karmazin

Lexi & Zelda Mid Life Mysteries

The Case of the Kona Curse

COPYRIGHT © 2025 by Emily Karmazin

Cover Art by *Teddi Black*

The Wild Rose Press, Inc.
PO Box 708
Adams Basin, NY 14410-0708
Visit us at www.thewildrosepress.com

Publishing History
First Edition, 2025
Trade Paperback ISBN 978-1-5092-6112-3
Digital ISBN 978-1-5092-6113-0

Lexi & Zelda Mid Life Mysteries
Published in the United States of America

Chapter One

"Didn't I mention it's a tour, Lexi?" Zelda asked, her face scrunched into a frown. She hadn't told me about yet one more tour she'd scheduled for us while we devoured wine coolers and Maui Onion potato chips last night. It was now morning, and I was barely awake. "The bus picks us up out front of the hotel in fifteen minutes. They provide snacks, waters, and drinks. And we can relax between stuff. Isn't that fun?"

"Hmph." I favored her with a side eye and took the last bit of passion fruit pastry, debating about going back to the breakfast buffet for another serving of bacon.

My best friend since grade school had planned out every minute of our three-week Hawaiian vacation, and so far, the plans left little breathing room. This was our first real vacation in years. Four days into the festivities, little of our time had been spent on the beach. It didn't appear like today would be any different. Forgoing the extra bacon slices, we finished breakfast and sauntered through the hotel to the front lobby.

Pristine white stone floors led through spacious and quiet corridors lined with tasteful, understated tropical art. No bright colors here. Even the lighting was muted. Stone floors opened to paths lined with lush gardens and serene pools. A cool breeze ran through from the ocean, rustling the vacationer's light clothing as they ran and bustled about. Cars, share drivers, and tour buses of various sizes lined the cobblestone road.

Zelda glanced around before marching in the direction of a smaller bus parked at the end of the circle drive. "There it is. Come on."

A tall, well-built man wearing a blinding magenta polo with khaki shorts asked, "You ladies joining us on the Volcanoes Adventures?" The shorts bordered on indecently short, but I wasn't offended by the display of tan thighs.

Zelda bounced to a stop in front of him. "Yes, for two." She rummaged in her hip pack, pulled out paper tickets, and gave him an ear-to-ear grin.

"*E Komo Mai!*" He took the paper, waved his arm like he was directing kids to their deaths in the chocolate factory, and bellowed, "All aboard!"

"Aloha!" Zelda squealed and ran up the steps. "Isn't this fun?"

My eyes rolled back in my head as I followed her up the steps, and my heart started to flutter. I forced myself to shake off the sensations of anxiety and impending doom. What could go wrong on a gorgeous Hawaiian tour?

Ever since a serial killer had kidnapped and held me captive several months back, I'd been on a cocktail of muscle relaxants, anti-depressives, high-power analgesics, and sleep meds. As a nurse, I grasped the concept that pills could help, but I also knew the side effects could easily outweigh the benefits. This whole trip was about feeling better and leaving the past, as well as medications, behind. I made a mental note to check in with the doctor as soon as we returned home.

I dropped in the cushioned seat next to Zelda and sighed. She was leaning over the back of the seat, already in conversation with the man behind us. He appeared to be close to our ages, maybe a few years younger. "Lexi, this is Jeff. He's staying here at the Orchid Hokulea, too. Isn't that fun?"

"Sure is, Zel. Nice to meet you." I nodded to the perfectly coiffed, blond-haired Jeff. He returned my greeting with an absent-minded wave.

Between the two of us, Zelda was more of the free spirit, and I knew she was trying her damnedest to make sure I forgot the troubles left back home in Atherton, Missouri. But if every time we did anythingand she asked if it was fun, I was going to kill her, then leave her body in the lava fields for the wild goats.

A squeal of the sound system put my jagged nerves on a sharper edge. "Oh, for fu—"

The tour leader, the same guy in the magenta shirt and skin-tight shorts, slipped on a headset and didn't have to work very hard for my attention. "*Hey, hey, Aloha kakahiaka*! That's a good morning to all of my mainland friends. Anyone from the islands?"

He glanced around the group, but no one moved. "No? Great, then I can tell you all of my tall tales and you won't be the wiser." He paused for light laughter. "I'm Koa and I'll be your guide. This is Sam." Koa motioned to a rotund fellow sitting behind the driver's seat. He turned slightly and gave a wave. "On this tour, we're going to explore, see, and learn about the largest active volcano in the world. And have a safe amount of fun. Who's up for some good times, uh?"

A smattering of cheers, and even I joined in, his enthusiasm contagious. "Great, I'll be giving facts and chatting along the road. Yell out questions." With that, he settled into the seat and the engine roared to life.

Still on her knees, Zelda was still leaning over the back of the seat, chatting with Jeff. I smacked her on the rear end. "Sit down like an adult."

She dropped into the seat with a sly smirk. "This is better than us trying to go it alone." She patted my arm. "You can relax and don't have to worry about anything."

I gave her a warm smile, not having the heart to tell her all I wanted was to lie on the beach and soak in the warming sunshine. As it was, I was happy for the air conditioning and comfy seat.

We pulled out of the parking lot a few minutes later and the narration began. Koa's inflection was warm, and he had an animated style that was engaging. Once on the main highway, we passed the lava fields that covered both sides of the road, black rock stretching from the ocean to the mountains. Along the roadway, bright pink and red flower bushes lent pops of color to the ebony landscape.

"The lava fields surrounding us are around a hundred and fifty years old. Some are over a thousand years old," Koa said. "These aren't just geological features but a deep part of our Hawaiian heritage. Pele, the volcano Goddess, is credited for the lava flow you see. Eruptions are displays of her temper. Now, Pele, like all women, isn't one-sided, but complex. She's both a creator and a destroyer…"

I found myself enthralled by the comforting tone of his voice and the deep legends of the place. By the time we arrived at Volcanoes National Park, I couldn't wait to get out off the bus and see the steam vents and sacred spots. Zelda disappeared with Jeff, the guy from behind us, without a backwards glance. I wondered if we were on this tour more so she could spend time with him than to sightsee. Hours later, after exploring the rugged coastline and lava tubes buried in tropical foliage, my legs were so sore, I could barely manage the steps that led to the parking lot. Once we boarded the bus, I dozed off.

I woke just as we pulled into a small parking lot that was just big enough for our tour bus and a few cars. "Folks, we have a treat for you. We're the only tour that comes to this museum, and in fact, you must be a historian or indigenous to get access." Koa directed Sam to angle the bus along the side of a small, one-story building. "But we here at Lava Lovin' Tours, we have special access."

"What makes it so special?" another tourist asked. This one sat close to the front and had had more than her fair share of complimentary snacks and canned cocktails.

"It is home to the Wai Ola artifact, a gift to Pele from Kanaloa, the ocean god," Koa said. "It means living water, and legend has it the owner is granted eternal life. But that's impossible because we don't believe in ownership like that." Koa shrugged. "Either way, it's a rare piece of early Hawaiian history that few people have the chance to see."

Oohs and ahhs filled the bus. We filed out like kids on a field trip and with a similar level of excitement. Before I knew it, Zelda was off with Jeff again.

The museum interior was as simple as the exterior, with all of the attention on the artifact and displays on Hawaiian history. I frowned as Zelda's giggle echoed through the space. It wasn't like her to ignore a museum, she loved history. After exploring, I made my way back to the bus and knocked on the door.

Koa had a sandwich in his hand as he opened the door. "Hey, are you good?"

"Yeah, just wanting to sit and rest for a while. Is that okay?" I could have found a bench in the museum to sit on, but I wanted the quiet of an empty bus.

He nodded. "Sure, sure. Come on." I felt his gaze on me as I passed him, and I dropped into my seat with a sigh. Sensing his nearness, I glanced up to find him standing in front of me with a small cooler in one hand. "Hey, have a sandwich? I've got some sweets if you'd rather have that."

I shook my head, but my stomach growled. "Thanks."

Koa smiled and took the seat across the aisle, the khaki shorts straining against muscular thighs. The cooler held a couple of plastic wrapped sandwiches, small cakes, fruit, and bags of chips. My stomach rumbled again.

He handed me a sandwich and a bag of chips. "Hold on, I've got some water up front." He sat the cooler down in the aisle and came back with a wet bottle of water and paper towels. "Here."

"Thank you." I took the items, sitting everything in the seat next to me. Unwrapping the sandwich, I took a bite and considered Koa watching me. I chewed, enjoying the meat, cheese, and bread combination before inquiring, "What? Is there something on my face or do you just like to watch women eat?"

He laughed, and a warm shiver traveled through me. "No, just it's rare to see a mainlander enjoy Spam as much as you seem to."

I shrugged. "It's delicious." I took another bite. The

only sound between us was our chewing and rustling of containers and napkins. I finished the sandwich and chips in record time and wiped my mouth with a napkin, eyeing the fruit and cakes in the cooler.

Koa took in my enjoyment. "Help yourself, my dear."

Without hesitation, I reached for the small cakes and popped the lid. The creaminess of coconut wafted out. I picked the piece up with my fingers and took a bite. The cake was lush and creamy. I nodded and chewed my satisfaction.

"Coconut Tres Leches." Koa's face scrunched into a crooked grin. "Kind of. That's what my aunty calls it anyway." He opened the lid on a bowl of pineapple chunks and dug in. "Are you feeling better?"

I finished the bite. "Yes, thanks. Never underestimate the healing powers of a good meal."

"Agreed. And nothing is better than a home-cooked meal. What brought you to the islands?"

I debated for a half second telling him my entire life story from birth. Something about him made me want to tell him everything. "My friend and I decided we needed a tropical vacation. The usual, a few weeks of sun, ocean, and good food."

Koa's gaze twinkled. "And some strong alcohol?"

"A bit." I laughed breathlessly. Another reason to cut back on the prescription medications was to be able to safely enjoy a powerful drink. I wiped my mouth and bundled my trash together. "Thanks again. Are you from the islands?"

Koa wrapped up his trash and bent to return the containers to the cooler. "Yeah, I was born here." He clicked the lid closed. "But I moved to the mainland for college and ended up staying for a while. Just came back recently. I—" He was interrupted by banging at the door. "Excuse me, duty calls." With a smile, he opened the door just as Zelda and Jeff burst in.

They bounded up the stairs. "Oh no, did we wake you?" Zelda asked before sliding next to me. Jeff dropped into the seat behind us.

"Nope, did you learn a lot?" Zelda recently left teaching history and English at our local high school and could spend days in even the smallest of museums. The fact she was the first on the bus gave me pause.

Zelda's forehead wrinkled in thought. "Yeah, yeah. Lots of good stuff." Her fisted on the arm rest, the knuckles sheet white.

"What's happening?" I asked, my mouth dry and voice cracking.

Zelda dug out a bottle of water and passed it to me, keeping her eyes in front. I shook the water bottle already in my hand in front of her face. She ignored me. Something was up, and I was pretty sure she was involved.

I stood, stretched, walked to the front of the bus, and threw my trash away. Koa leaned over the steering wheel, his attention focused on a gathering of uniformed individuals who stood outside the museum entrance. I bent down to get a better view through the windshield.

"Probably some *haole* doing something stupid," he commented.

I gave him a questioning look.

"*Haole*. Usually a tourist doing something stupid," he explained.

Sam's round form emerged from the center of the group and strode toward the bus. Koa got out of his seat and met him outside. His face darkened as Sam spoke. Something had happened. Slowly, the rest of the tourists filed out of the museum like ghosts.

Koa jumped up the steps into the bus. For one of the first times in months, my senses began to sing with energy. "Koa, I'm a nurse. Does anyone need help?"

His gaze met mine and the hardness in his eyes made my breath catch. He leaned in close. "No injuries. Seems like something is missing from the museum."

A pleasant warmth spread through me that had nothing to do with a potential crime, but his proximity. I cursed. I'm a forty-something woman, not a teenager, and way too old for crushes. He motioned for me to go back to my seat as the rest of the group filed on. Sam brought up the rear.

Just as I was debating about asking to get off the bus and find a bathroom, Sam cleared his throat and took the headset mike from Koa. "Folks, if I may have your attention for a bit." He cleared his throat again. "As you may have heard, an artifact is missing from the museum. A very important one. If you or anyone in your party was involved, please return the item, or tell us what you know. I've got cards here to pass out, and we'll have to share our guest list with the police." He motioned to the patrol cars arriving in the parking lot. "Any help is appreciated." Sam handed the mic to Koa but stopped and turned back. Something about that turn caused my blood to run cold.

"One more thing, folks…I understand you all are tourists here and don't appreciate the ways of the island. Removing items from Pele's Garden is opening yourself up for a curse." He shook his head, and his face darkened. "You all might think that's all superstition and whatnot, but I've been here long enough to tell you there's truth to it. I've seen enough to know even removing the smallest piece of Aina is bad luck." He rested his stare on each of us. When it landed on Zelda and me, my breath caught in my throat from its intensity. "Take care of yourselves."

With those ominous words, he handed the mic to Koa and dropped into the seat, removed a handkerchief from his pocket and wiped his brow. The bus was quiet as Sam pulled away and angled to the main road. I spared a glance at Zelda. She looked ashen, and her eyes had wrinkled to slits. I'd seen that look a handful of times in our lives. Usually right before she was arrested at a protest or ran into a horrible student's parent at the grocery store.

If there was trouble, more often than not, Zelda would find it. Usually, it was fighting for an underdog because she had a good heart and a developed sense of right and wrong, but occasionally, she bet on the wrong horse.

My heart dropped to my feet. "Oh hell, Zelda, what did you do?"

Chapter Two

As Zelda whipped around to face me, her glare held daggers. "Why do you assume I've done something?"

I pursed my lips, noticing she didn't deny the accusation. A simple deflection, but one we both were good at when wanting to avoid the truth. "I'm going to ask again, what did you do?" My tone was harder than it needed to be.

Her eyes widened. Thirty years of friendship, and she knew exactly what the tone implied. "I didn't *do* anything." She dropped her head to my shoulder, her lips close to my ear. "But I *might* have seen something."

I pulled back to study her face. She was telling the truth. "You need to tell the authorities what you *might* have seen," I said. "Before anything else happens. I don't want to worry about the police and whatever else. Heaven knows your never-ending tours are enough."

She pulled away from me and leaned against the window with a loud sniff. "I will. We don't have that much going on." Her chin raised. "I want to make sure we see everything, especially before your parents show up."

I sighed from the frustration flowing through my veins and zapping my energy. I love my parents, but my shoulders tensed just thinking about their arrival on the island. They thought joining us on *our* Hawaiian vacation was a fabulous idea and I couldn't say no. All of a sudden, the bus felt like a prison, and I needed to move.

"Zel, we have three weeks. On one island. We have the time, and I want to rest, okay?" I grabbed her hand and intertwined our fingers. "You need to rest too, whether or not you want to. Whatever is planned for tomorrow, let's cancel."

She squeezed my hand back and added a shake. "I don't know how we can do that though. Tomorrow is a beach day, and so is the day after." Her tone mocking. "I guess we could just lie in bed all day if we have to cancel…"

I gave her a playful push and we both laughed, breaking the tension. "As long as we're lying somewhere, I'll be a happy girl."

"I've been an asshole lately, sorry." She rubbed her forearm against mine. For Zelda, that was a huge and rare apology.

I rubbed my arm against hers. "Yeah, more than usual, but I still love you."

We leaned against each other and fell into a light sleep, lulled by the rocking of the bus and the low chatter of the other tourists. The bus came to a jerky stop, and I opened my eyes. Zelda was awake and stretching, ready for the next adventure.

Zelda again disappeared quickly, leaving me alone. I was eager to be out of my seat and onto the beach. As I wandered the black sand, the warmth and softness of the grains surprised me. I went to my knees and buried my hands to my wrists. For a moment, everything about the past few months faded. The tourists and their noise felt far away and unobtrusive. The only thing left was the rhythmic sounds of the surf and the birds in the nearby forest.

Without warning, a shrill, straggled scream pierced the serenity. Zelda ran out of the woods that edged the beach with Jeff stumbling behind her. Something dark dripped across her T-shirt.

"Zelda!" I screamed, struggling against the sand. She collapsed next to me, her breath in gasps as Jeff ran past us holding his face, blood streaming down his chest. "What happened?"

My gaze searched her for injuries, but I didn't find any. Memories of another female, covered in blood, flashed through my mind and I squeezed my eyes shut, pushing the images aside.

"Jeff…we were in the forest," she gasped. "Something attacked him."

I gripped her by the shoulders and gave her a hard shake. "You okay, nothing got you?"

"Yeah…yeah…I just don't know what happened." Her voice sounded far away.

I gave her shoulder another shake before pulling her up and guiding her back to the bus. At the edge of the parking lot, we met up with Koa and Sam. Jeff stood between them, looking dazed and bloody.

Sam held out his beefy arm to push me aside. "Stand aside, ma'am."

I pushed his arm down. "No, I'm a nurse. What happened here?"

One local who took in the scene had a huge smile on his face. "This one got into it with a Big Island Cat, didn't you, bro?" Laughter tinged in each word as he pointed at Jeff.

The humor was lost on me. Koa spoke. "Seems he tried to pet some feral cat, and it thanked him with a couple of claws to the face. You know head wounds bleed like a stuck pig."

I nodded and swallowed the knot in my throat.

"He's lucky he didn't get shot," another local piped up. "Doesn't that part of the beach belong to Cregg?"

The first local spat on the ground. "Naw, bro. Cregg might own a lot, but never the beach, bro. Never."

My gaze darted between the two, trying to pick up on who or what Cregg was, and what they were talking about. Koa groaned under his breath, pulling my focus back to the injured man. Whatever was going on, there wasn't time for it now.

"Let's get the first aid kit," I said, redirecting Koa's attention. "I'll get him cleaned up and bandaged for the rest of the drive."

Koa didn't answer but stalked toward the bus. "Good, thanks. It'll still be a couple of hours back to Kona. I could drop him here at the local clinic, but the boss will kill me. A private driver will charge out the ass to get him back to the hotel."

"No worries, I got it." I followed Koa as he led a dazed Jeff by the arm onto the bus and into his seat. Koa handed me the first aid kit and left the bus. Crisis managed. I was envious of the nonchalant way they handled the situation.

While Jeff sat, blood trickling from his head, I opened the kit, ripped open a couple packages of gauze and a bottle marked antiseptic. "Hey, Jeff, do you remember me? My friend Zelda and I sit in front of you on the bus." Pouring a bit of the liquid on the pads, I moved to dab it on his face. "I'm a nur—"

He recoiled from my touch. Contempt and scorn oozed from him. "What the hell are you doing?"

I dropped my hand and pretended to be busy with something in the kit. "I'm Lexi; we met on the bus earlier today. I'm a nurse, and I'll get you fixed up before we get going." I finished the mental count to fifty, so I didn't throttle him and picked up the gauze again. "Can I clean you up so we can get you to a hospital?"

He appeared calmer, so I moved closer, but he slapped my hand away. "This isn't my first animal attack."

I sank back into the seat, dropped the gauze into the kit and crossed my arms against my chest. I counted to a hundred before I spoke, giving both of us time. "A feral cat may, or may not, harbor over fifty different bacteria and parasites." I counted to twenty, letting my words sink in, before continuing. "One scratch may, or may not, contain many dangerous pathogens." I counted to ten. "It is in your best interest to allow me to clean your wounds to mitigate those pathogens or infections from gaining a hold." I didn't count this time but favored him with a sad, knowing smile. "If they haven't already."

It took less than a count of five for Jeff to decide. "Fine, but be careful. If you mess up, I'll sue you for malpractice."

I resisted rolling my eyes, picked up the gauze, and cleaned the wounds, ignoring his dramatic hissing of pain. It wasn't the first time I had been threatened with a lawsuit. If he was going to be dumb enough to pet a feral cat in the woods, that's on him. But he didn't strike me as the animal lover type, in fact, the exact opposite. But to act like a snob when someone was offering him help was another thing. I cleaned and bandaged the wounds without another word.

The entire process, including his hissy fit, took less

than ten minutes. I moved to clean up the first aid kit when he opened his mouth again. "Are you done?" His voice was that of a petulant child.

"Sure am."

I didn't even look up from the kit as I reorganized and closed it. I walked the kit to the front of the bus and felt his eyes burn a hole in my back. This wasn't the first time a patient was rude and wouldn't be the last. Ungrateful brat, and at his age he should know to act better. I shook my head. Some people never learned.

Needing space, I stepped off the bus and took a deep breath of the fresh air. Koa appeared, leaning against the side of the bus. "Will the Prince survive?"

I rolled my eyes and stretched my back. "For the moment, his injuries are superficial. No stitches needed." I joined him, leaning against the bus. "He doesn't need to go to the emergency room. He'll be fine if he monitors it to make sure it doesn't get an infection."

His face scrunched. "We don't have rabies here on the island."

"And that sounds eerily like something a lawyer would have said in a resurrected monster movie, right before a dinosaur ripped them off the toilet."

Koa laughed. Full-on laughter. "Good one, lady. But really, no rabies on the island."

My cheeks felt like they were on fire. "The name is Lexi."

"Okay, Lexi." He sounded the words out like he was tasting my name. I resisted a shiver as he held out his hand. "I'm Koa, your trusty tour guide. Nice to officially meet you."

I held out my hand, and he wrapped his around mine. "Nice to meet you." I didn't want to take my hand away, but did. "Even so, there's a thing called cat scratch fever. And as much as I'd like to see Prince Jeff withering in agony, he needs to be watchful. Unfortunately, his attitude does not inspire confidence."

"Good, good. I'll make sure he understands."

We walked back towards the beach, shoulder to shoulder, and I felt a long-buried, but familiar, stirring. Was it possible to have feelings for someone again? I hadn't thought it possible after everything I'd been through, but maybe I could at least entertain the idea.

Now that Jeff was taken care of, I needed to find Zelda. "Did you see my friend? The one with the curls?"

"And the fanny pack and more fun facts about the island than I have?" Koa mimicked Zelda's tone of fun. I laughed, and it felt so good. "Yeah, Sam took her down to the beach. She's fine, just stained clothes, but the resort has laundry so it should wash out."

I nodded. If I knew anything, it was how to get blood out of clothes. I pushed the thought aside and continued walking with Koa. We found Zelda sitting on the sand with Sam. His arms moving in an animated story that had her holding her belly as she laughed.

Koa smiled, and it warmed me. "You telling tall tales again, Uncle?" he asked Sam, giving him a playful smack on the back.

Sam turned, returning the smile. "Hey, I gotta keep the ladies laughing."

"Always. We have to get on the road." Koa helped Sam to stand, then assisted Zelda to her feet before she and Sam walked arm and arm back to the bus.

Back at the bus, a small crowd of tourists surrounded Jeff as he recounted his horrifying ordeal. Koa and I stood off to the side, listening. To hear him tell it, he survived a run-in with a tiger. I had to suppress my laughter as I glanced around the crowd of ohhing and ahhing people.

Zelda appeared at my side. "All for a damn cat."

"Enough of the prince holding court," Koa muttered, before stepping towards the group. "All right, folks, time to load. Head on back to the resort." He waved his arms in big circles towards the bus. The crowd dissipated and moved onto the bus. Jeff held his head like he'd taken a baseball bat to it rather than a cat paw. I suppressed a laugh as he walked past me to take his seat. Zelda was seated already, deep into her cell phone, unconcerned about her new friend's condition.

Did she see him for the drama queen he was or was there more there? It wasn't like her not be concerned about someone's well-being. Hell, a year ago, she'd fought to the death for a former student. I sighed and threw a sidelong glance at her. Something wasn't adding up here.

Within minutes Koa closed the door, before Sam pulled out of the parking lot to head home.

Chapter Three

"Let's get in the water before the sun sets."

Warm waves of azure colored water tickled my toes, releasing a tightness deep inside me. The ocean pulled the sand from under my feet; the world slipped away with each grain of sand. Sighing, I closed my eyes. This was the part of the vacation I had waited for. It was a perfect end to the eventful day of the Volcanoes tour.

Zelda's hand wrapped around mine and tugged. I opened my eyes to find her smile as bright as the setting sun. "Come on! The ocean is waiting for you, babe." She pulled me the rest of the way in, releasing my hand as a cool wave crashed into my stomach.

She dived in and popped back up, shaking water from her curls and laughing. "Isn't this better than tornado season back home?"

I agreed. The Hawaiian beach won out over Midwestern storms and tornadoes any day. A glance around ensured the other tourists were out of earshot. "So, are you going to tell me what you saw on the tour?"

Zelda's face turned into a frown. "That guy, Jeff? He stole the artifact." I stared, open-mouthed as she gave her head of curls a nonchalant toss. "I didn't see him do it *exactly,* but he was trying to get me to create a distraction in the museum and he had something in his pocket, like a hunk of tinfoil, that he kept showing me. But I have no idea why."

My arms and legs danced in the water as I processed the information. "That's how he got around the security system? With whatever that stuff was?" Jeff was more than an annoying guy, he was also bad news. It wasn't my place to tell Zelda that. She wouldn't listen anyway. My friend is a woman who had to come to her own realizations.

"I think so. I…I promise I'll take care of it and make it right. First thing in the morning, I'll call the park rangers. Their card said the office was closed by the time we got back to the resort anyway."

Zelda always kept her word and didn't throw promises around lightly. The problem was that even though she had the best of intentions, things often got out of control. I pushed the idea aside. If I can't trust my best friend, who can I trust? The coolness soothed my tight muscles, and I took a deep breath and slid under, letting the water cover my head. I spat water as I came up. "Remind me, what do we have planned for tomorrow?" I vaguely remember her telling me earlier in the day, but the actual plans escaped me.

Zelda treaded water, her dark hair bathed in golden light from the sun setting. "I figured we'd take a break for a few days. Even if that means no more Mr. Mustache."

Despite the coolness of the water, warmth rose in my face. Koa, our most recent tour guide, bore a striking resemblance to a certain television crime solver from back in the eighties, and I had developed a ridiculous crush on him in a short amount of time. But…after a recent breakup with my long-time boyfriend, I wasn't in the market for a vacation romance, or any other type. Even if he's handsome, funny, and polite.

I shook the idea out of my head. "Whatever, Zel."

"Hmm…it didn't seem like whatever when he made you laugh." She winked. "More than once?"

"So, what—beach time tomorrow?" I inquired, trying to distract her, and failing.

"And happy hour. I saw a Samurai Slinger on the beach bar menu. I must try."

We got out of the water and trudged onto the beach, fighting for footing against the pull of the waves. As we dropped onto the low beach chairs, the last rays of the sunset disappeared, throwing light on the very tops of the waves.

At peace, when my phone dinged, I didn't hesitate to pick it up.

"Mr. Mustache?" Zelda playfully kicked me from her chair.

I frowned. "And how would he have my number?" A glance at the home screen showed a text message.

"I think I had to put our info in on the registration." Zelda sighed and rested her wrists on her head. "He could get it from there."

"More likely you slipped it to him. It's my mom."

I loved my parents, but both of them had become a handful since retiring a few years ago and moving to Florida. It had been my parent's dream, but neither seemed to enjoy it.

—Hawaii is amazing!!! Can't wait to see you both!—

The message ended with random emojis that I hoped my mom didn't understand, since I was confident it was a sexual proposition.

"Are they on their way or have they done something else?" Zelda asked with a sigh. My parents, on an around the world cruise, had decided to take a break and join us in Hawaii.

"Not sure, I thought they'd be joining us soon, but the text reads like they're already here." I showed the phone to Zelda. She rolled her eyes after reading it. "No actual dates or times of arrival." I dropped the phone in my tote. "They still could change their plans, but they'll probably pop up somewhere random."

"You know, since they retired, I think the best way to describe them is two teenagers with too much time and money. Your parents are a hoot, and you're one hundred percent right."

Relaxing in the lounge chair, I pushed worry about my parents out of the way. Zelda had it nailed. I wondered what trouble they could get into on the island and quickly pushed the item away as my heart rate sped up. The last thing we needed was a pair of geriatric teenagers thrown into the mix while we're trying to relax.

We stayed on the beach until the breeze dried our skin. Back in the room, I showered and resolved that tomorrow would be a new day. I would forget about my tour guide crush and focus on relaxing and getting a tan. After a dinner of bagged salad, rotisserie chicken, and pineapple rum spritzes, Zelda and I talked about nothing and everything until I dozed off in the chair.

"Come on, Lex." Zelda patted my shoulder. "Go on to bed."

I yawned and stood with a groan. "But I want to stay up and keep you company."

She laughed. "Don't worry about me. I'm a big girl. I'll find ways to entertain myself." Zelda helped me to bed, tucking me into warm blankets with the cool, ocean breeze blowing in from the open sliders. With a sigh of contentment, I fell into a deep slumber.

****

A scream shattered my rest. As images of previous horrors flashed before my eyes, I was out of bed, running for Zelda.

Throwing open her bedroom door, I flipped on the overhead light. Shadows filled the room from the low-wattage bulb and the rotating ceiling fan. Zelda sat in the bed wearing an oversized T-shirt that was covered in blood.

Next to her was a body.

"Lexi…" she whispered before breaking into a sob.

I hesitated at the doorway not wanting to disturb anything, but someone was injured, and my nursing instinct took over. "Zelda, are you okay?"

She glanced down at the dried brown stains on her shirt, eyes widened.

"F that." I continued to the other side of the bed and pulled back enough of the blood-soaked covers. A nude man lay there. The body was already stiff and starting to discolor. A quick check for a pulse told me he was long dead. The multiple stab wounds littering his graying flesh meant I didn't need to question the cause of death. "Zelda, what happened?"

When I got no response, I scrambled around to her side of the bed and grabbed her by the shoulders. "Zelda, Zelda. Can you understand me?"

Her eyes were blank and her skin pale, shock setting in. Her pulse was fast, and her chest rose and fell in a quick, uneven rhythm. I did a quick body scan to make sure she wasn't injured before grabbing her cell phone off the nightstand.

"Hi, yeah, this is Lexi—Alexandra Burns. I'm staying at Hokulea Shores, room 419. I've got a medical emergency and need immediate assistance." I glanced over at the blood stains. "And the police. Definitely the police."

I hung up and dropped the phone on the nightstand, then dragged Zelda into the living room and deposited her on the couch. I tucked pillows beneath her legs and wrapped a throw blanket around her before going to prop open the condo's front door.

It wasn't long before the sounds of multiple heavy footsteps in the hall approached. "Hawaii County Police," a cautious voice said on the other side of the door. "Officer Martel."

"We're here," I responded, as I sat next to Zelda's feet with my hands on my knees. My mind raced as I tried to remember all the things I learned watching true crime. Now, none of it seemed useful.

A dark uniformed arm pushed the door the rest of the way open, revealing a balding man with a middle-age pudge. "How are you doing this morning, ma'am?"

"I've been better. I'm Alexandra, and this is my friend Zelda. She's in shock and needs medical attention."

Martel stepped into the room. "An ambulance is on its way. You two the only ones here?"

"There's a body in the bedroom on your right." The matter-of-fact tone in my voice concerned me. How quickly I had gotten comfortable with death.

His hand rested near the weapon at his waist. "All right. We're just going to check that out." The doorway filled with uniformed officers. "If you'll stay put there, ma'am." He gave a small nod in the direction of the door, and an officer moved toward Zelda's room and entered. "Just one body, ma'am?"

I swallowed and my mouth felt full of dust. "Yeah, just the one." Wanting to ask, how many bodies should there be, officer? I suppressed a giggle.

The officer returned and, at the slight nod of his head, people went into a flurry of activity, moving quickly and efficiently in and out of the small condo. I heard low voices, saw the sidelong glances at Zelda and me as the officers formed a plan and a list of questions. A glance at Zelda's still pale face told me it would be a while before she would be able to answer anything.

The appearance of paramedics pulled me out of my thoughts. They assessed Zelda and got her ready to be transported but not before handcuffing her to the gurney. I bit my tongue. No one had any idea what had happened yet, but it felt like they were in a big hurry to secure her.

"We'll make sure she's restrained, sir," a paramedic with full arm tattoos said to Martel.

I cleared my throat and crossed my arms, staring hard at the officer. Hotel security stood just outside the door, looking grossly out of place among the various dark uniformed officers in their bright-colored polo shirts and Bermuda shorts. The medical examiner and the crime scene team arrived together. Their voices low. It seemed like forever before anyone would talk with me.

"Can I get you a drink, ma'am? Water?" Officer Martel asked.

"Can I get it myself?" My tone was more defiant than I wanted it.

His eyebrows raised. "No, I'll get it for you." He brought back a bottled water from the fridge in the other room, then squatted down in front of me, a notebook open in his hands. "How long have you been on the island?"

My attention was pulled away as the body was wheeled out on a gurney. On top of the navy body bag was a floral cover, which felt too cheery for the scene. I glanced back at Martel. How had he ended up here? How did anyone end up in paradise? Was it paradise if you spent your days interrogating middle-aged women at crime scenes?

"Thank you." I unscrewed the lid and drank. The water soothed the dryness in my mouth. "A few days."

The officer cleared his throat. "You moved the woman, is that right?"

I nodded. "Her name is Zelda, and yes. She was in shock, and I wanted to get her to a safe place."

He bounced on his heels. "That's fine. Besides that, did you touch anything?"

I replayed the events in my mind. "I hit the light switch because it was dark in the room before I moved to Zelda. When I saw the body, I pulled back the comforter to take the man's pulse. I think that's it."

He scribbled a few notes on the pad. "Okay, we're going to need your clothes. Officer Akana will assist."

I glanced down at myself. No blood or anything I could see on my pioneer style nightgown. Either way, there was no reason to argue. From my experience, it was best to go along with law enforcement…until it wasn't.

"Is there a place besides that room where have clothes?"

"Yeah, my room is there." I motioned behind me, stood, and Officer Akana followed. In my bedroom, she took my nightgown and bagged it. She closed the door as she left me to change.

I stood in the middle of the rented room, feeling lost and listening to the voices and the routines of any crime investigation from the other side of the door. Someone had died, violently, not that far from where I slept. I struggled to gulp air. If I didn't move soon, I would stay frozen forever. I shook my arms and legs to dispel the stagnant energy. I threw on shorts and a T-shirt over a sports bra and panties, making my bed and straightening the few personal items before setting out. At the last minute, I threw a similar set of clothes into my tote for Zelda. Back in the bathroom, I splashed my face with cool water and brushed my hair into a high ponytail, the waves and baby hairs already frizzy.

Taking a deep breath, I walked back into the living room. A hotel security officer stood next to Martel. They turned as I entered. "How are you feeling?" Martel inquired.

I grimaced. Frozen, locked up, confused, just great? Pick one. "When can I check on my friend?"

"The paramedics took her to the hospital. You should be able to meet her there. The forensic team has a couple hours left here. We'll need to get your statement, but once we do that and you promise not to leave the island, you should be free to move about."

"Can we do the statement now? I'm worried about her."

"I'd rather take the formal at the station, but we can get started now." He flipped open the notebook and pulled out the pen. "Can you tell me what happened?"

He took the seat on the sectional next to the security guard. His name tag read "Director Keawe," but he didn't introduce himself. Probably wasn't often he had to deal with a homicide.

I took the seat catty corner to them and leaned forward, debating how much to say. Less is more. "I don't know what to tell you."

"How about we start with what you did yesterday?"

"We did a tour yesterday of Volcanoes National Park and got back around dinner time."

His direct stare bore through me. "To clarify, who are *we*?"

"Zelda and myself."

"And how do you know each other?"

A nervous laugh escaped me. How to summarize almost forty years of friendship? "We grew up together and have been friends since." I left it at that, and he motioned for me to continue. "We're from Atherton, a small town in Missouri."

"How long are you here? Visiting any other islands?"

"Three weeks. No, just the Big Island."

"Good, good. You will not want to leave the island until all of this is cleared up. What did you all do when you got back from the tour?"

"We changed our clothes, sauntered to the beach, and stayed there until after sunset. Then we came back to the room, had dinner, and I fell asleep."

His blond brows pulled together. "You both came back to the room, and that's it?"

I swallowed hard. "Until I heard Zelda scream. I ran into her room and saw the body. I checked for vitals, then called emergency services. The rest is on record."

"Did you notice if your friend left the room or if anyone came in?"

I sipped the water. "I mean...I noticed the dead

body in her bed so one or the other happened."

His gaze narrowed. "That's it?"

I fidgeted with the hem of my shorts, finding a loose thread, and played with it between my fingers. Before I left Atherton, I had weaned myself off most of the medications from the recent injuries. Not the best idea for a nurse to do without a doctor's order, but I did it. The one medication I still took was a sleeping pill. It helped keep the nightmares away. I didn't want to admit I had taken anything, but it would come out if the investigation progressed. "I'm on medication for an injury back home. I notice little once I get to sleep."

"Uh, so that's it?" His tanned forehead wrinkled. "You all did a tour, came home, swam, and then fell asleep. All sweet and nice, but you didn't recognize the man in the bed?"

I blinked and slouched, folding my arms on my legs. I had been so focused on doing things right, I didn't examine the face that closely. "I'm sorry, I'm a nurse. I wasn't looking at who it was, but what I could do to help. Once I didn't get a pulse, I moved on to Zelda and called 911. I can tell you it's a male, around forty, with brown hair, average weight, multiple stab wounds."

"So, you didn't recognize him? Is that what you're saying?"

I shook my head. "No, should I?"

The security officer's eyes widened, and he stared into mine. I wiggled in my seat, uncomfortable under his stare. He had yet to say a word, and his silence was worrying under my skin.

Martel stood with a huff, tucking the notebook in his uniform pocket. "If that's it, you're free to go. Just make sure you don't leave the island, even to go to Maui or

Oahu. Got it?"

I nodded and grabbed my tote by the door. Curiosity got the better of me and I turned back. "Real quick, can you tell me who the, uh…dead person is?"

Keawe's eyebrows raised as he spoke for the first time. "Jeff Knox. I'm surprised you didn't recognize him from your tour yesterday." He shrugged. "But I guess people look different naked and dead."

Chapter Four

"Jeff?"

Okay, so he'd sat behind us on the bus during the tour, then acted like the drama queen after the animal attack. He and Zelda had chatted often, but why would he be in Zelda's bed?

More important—why was he now dead?

The security officer's blue stare bore through me. "You seem surprised?"

"It's not every day I find someone dead in my best friend's bed."

Martel's gaze narrowed. "Hmm...remember what I said. Don't leave the island."

"And you'll be moved to another unit inside the hotel. Stop in at the front desk when you come back from checking on your friend," Keawe added, the tone no friendlier than Martel's.

I grabbed my tote and stumbled out, dodging officials. Housekeeping carts dotted the hallway, and additional hotel security officers stood off to the side, monitoring the activity.

Did Zelda meet up with Jeff last night while I slept? She was an adult and could do whatever she wanted, but why hadn't she told me? After knowing he'd stolen the artifact, why did she continue to associate with him? That wasn't like her at all.

In the hotel lobby, I shoved a handful of granola bars

and fruit into my tote with a bottled water from the snack bar before heading to the parking lot. The sheriff was right, the phone map showed one hospital on this side of the island. I drove through the resort as the first rays of morning sunlight washed the lush foliage.

Windows down and radio up, I used the short drive to clear my head. The hospital's white and green exterior wasn't much different from the community hospital I'd worked at back home, and I welcomed the familiarity. I checked in with the front desk to confirm I could see Zelda before I went back. A uniformed officer sat outside the curtained room at the end of the hall, with all of his attention on his cell phone.

I favored him with a curt nod as I approached but didn't slow. He stood, stretched, and barely glanced up from his phone. "You family?"

My hand resting on the curtain. "Yep." We'd been friends longer than most people were married, close enough. "Plus the folks at the front desk said I can go in."

"Okay, ma'am. Just don't slip her a weapon or anything." He sat again, his attention fully on his phone in less than ten seconds.

I snorted and pushed back the curtain to reveal Zelda propped up in the hospital bed. "Lexi!" She stretched her arms out to me, but the clink of metal pulled her left arm back. She sat handcuffed to the bed. I ran to her and wrapped my arms around her. She collapsed against me, sobbing.

"Oh my God, Zel." I didn't believe she would commit murder—unless someone hurt a person she loved, and then all bets were off. "What happened?"

Between sobs, she struggled with words. "I don't remember much." She pulled back, and I dug some tissues out of my bag. She blew her nose loudly. I settled onto the bed, holding her hand, and waited. "You saw Jeff was in my bed. Dead." A blush rose on her face.

"How did he get there?"

She shook her head. "I don't know."

I squeezed her hand. Zelda was the smartest person I knew, but also beyond trusting, especially with matters of the heart. "Did you meet with him last night?" I asked, massaging her hand.

She shook her head. "Yes, but not for sex. I wanted him to come clean and turn himself in. I told him I would go to the police anyway." Her voice rose with the last words.

"Shhh…watch your volume." I motioned over my shoulder to the officer's shadow on the other side of the curtain. Zelda nodded. "Did he say why he did it? Did anyone hear this conversation?"

"I don't know, we were in the hotel lounge, so maybe?" Her face scrunched as she thought back. "Something about a key to the fountain of youth?"

I scoffed. "Might have been a fountain of youth, but not a fountain of life." Clearing my throat, I continued. "So, what happened last night?"

"I told you I could entertain myself." A playful smile crossed her face and disappeared. "We met in the lounge for drinks. I told him he had to return the artifact. He said no, said something about it was too important." She bit her lip. "Something about making things right? I don't know, it makes little sense now. I remember I was warm, and the breeze was freezing, and I couldn't stop shivering. Then everything went dark, full of shadows. That's all I remember."

It sounded like someone, probably Jeff, had drugged

Zelda. I also knew about how police officials work. They don't always listen to plain citizens until it's too late.

"I believe you, Zel, but that doesn't mean the police will believe you're innocent. If you were in the resort lounge, that means people saw you together. Even if he hadn't been found in your bed, you'd still be a prime suspect."

"Fantastic. I slept with a criminal, which is not great, but I didn't kill him. That's a silver lining."

I recognized her tone. It was one step away from total denial. Zelda was in serious trouble. My head spun and sweat broke out all over my body that had nothing to do with the humidity. She was keeping secrets from me, and that would only lead her to getting thrown in prison. I squeezed her hand too hard. That wouldn't happen on my watch.

A too-chipper nurse in purple scrubs popped in with discharge paperwork and a small bag of medication. He talked fast, and I nodded, asking a few questions to confirm they had done a tox screen. Though Zelda had no obvious injuries, they'd treated her for shock. The small prescription bottle was for sleeping pills. I frowned. It was an odd choice for someone experiencing shock, and Zelda usually slept like the dead. I shoved them into the depths of my tote, never to be seen again.

Before I could inquire about the prescription, the nurse left with a bounce in his step, and I slid off the bed and pulled the blanket down. "Let's see if we can get you out of here, okay?"

She nodded and reached to remove the hospital gown, the cuff clinking against the bar. "We have a slight problem."

The curtain whipped open, and the officer stood

there, scowling at us both. "What do you think you're doing?"

"Getting dressed and leaving," I said, turning to face him. "Want to help?"

He rested his hands on his hips. "That's not going to happen. The suspect will need to stay here until she's released, and then I'll escort her to the station."

"She was released. Can't she just give you the statement now?"

The corners of his mouth lifted. "Statement? She'll do that once she's booked for murder."

Chapter Five

A loud sniff came from next to me. "Can I at least put panties on, or are you all going to drag me to the police station with my business hanging out?"

I resisted the urge to roll my eyes. It warmed my heart to have her feisty side back, but from the sour expression on the officer's face, it wasn't going over well. This wasn't our small town of Atherton where everyone knew everyone else.

"Well?" Zelda attempted to cross her arms with the handcuff in place and failed.

The officer approached and unlocked it. "Fine, get dressed, but do it fast." He turned to leave. "And no funny business." He left the curtain open as he conferred with the nurse.

"Like he would recognize funny business." I slammed the curtain closed and dug through my tote bag, pulling out a small stack of my clothes. Zelda eyed them as I handed them to her. "Put this on unless you *do* want the entire island to see your business."

She held up the T-shirt featuring the logo for a 5k race I ran a few years ago for the local hospital's pediatric wing fundraiser. "Oh, I can't wear this. One look will tell them I'm a liar." I threw the shorts at her head.

Zelda dressed, and the officer escorted her out to a waiting sheriff's car. I stood behind them and waved when the door slammed shut. The car drove away, and I remained behind, staring after them.

Filling my lungs with a deep breath, I made a mental list of things to do. First, breakfast. The granola bars in my tote would cover that. Second, sheriff's station. Third, find an attorney. Marching back to the rental car, it occurred to me that the worn T-shirt and shorts weren't the most appropriate outfit for official wear. On second thought, the first stop would be back at the resort to change clothes.

****

Back at the resort, the sheriff and security still had our condo blocked off with crime scene tape. As I wandered through the hotel lobby, the ocean breeze ruffled my hair and refreshed me. Guests meandered by, looking bright and tanned, voices sprinkled with laughter and shouts. A part of me wondered what it was like to not have a care in the world. Had it only been yesterday when my shoulders weren't up around my ears and my chest didn't feel like it was in a vise grip?

In the lobby seating area, I dropped into a wicker chair, pulled out my phone, and was searching for local criminal attorneys when someone sunk into the chair across from me.

"I just came back from a sunrise tour of Maunea Kea and was in the lobby when I heard security talking about a murder." Koa rested his forearms on his thighs. "Valet said they took Zelda out in an ambulance."

My heart skipped a beat as I took in his warm scent and concerned gaze. "You wouldn't happen to know a good criminal attorney, would you?"

His forehead raised. "I do, one of the best. You do, too."

I knew next to no one around here. "Who? Wait, you?"

"Hey, don't sound so surprised. But no, it's my cousin. You met him on the tour yesterday. Sam."

"Wait, Sam is a tour guide by day and attorney by night, or…?" Was this guy for real? Is he making a joke when my best friend was sitting at the police station? I resisted the urge to throttle him.

Koa gave a chuckle. "No, he's retired. Just does the tours so he doesn't annoy Aunty to death. Or the other way around."

I raised my palms. All my alarm bells were going off. "Wait, it's not that I'm not grateful, but what are the chances I just ran into you this morning? And your relative is an attorney?"

"What are the chances your best friend wakes up with a dead man in her bed?" he shot back.

My eyebrow rose. He was quick on his feet and smart. I liked that. Maybe too much. "*Touché.*"

"I grew up on this island. We're a small community. I have another cousin who's in the sheriff's office, and I know everyone." Koa leaned forward, and my breath caught. He raised his hand and rubbed my shoulder. "I can help. No worries."

Everything about him was calm and focused, but I couldn't shake the nagging feeling that him showing up was too easy, too convenient. I also couldn't shake my unwavering attraction to him. I crossed my arms and legs, wanting to put distance between us, but not push him away. Zelda did need help. "Sam is available?"

Koa nodded. "I think he's got the time. I'll text him and confirm. But first, what do you need? Do we need to get you some food?"

My stomach grumbled. The granola bar didn't seem as promising as whatever Koa had to offer. "Food would be fantastic."

He gave me a wink before he stood. "Come with me. There's a perfect place to grab a bite, and it's on the way to the police station."

With him so close, I couldn't decide if the butterflies in my stomach were a warning or attraction. Over forty and still didn't know my body. Fantastic. I veered towards the concierge stand to check on when the room was ready and let them know I'd be back in a few hours. The concierge confirmed the new room would be ready in a couple hours and didn't blink when I asked if the lobby had cameras. If the butterflies were a warning, the cameras would catch Koa and me leaving together. Just in case he was planning on throwing me into the ocean. And most importantly, they would show what happened to Zelda last night in the lounge. I made a note to follow up on the cameras.

Outside, I was already covered in a layer of perspiration. It didn't bother me so much when we were doing something fun, but now things were serious, and the heat was oppressive. In the valet area, he waved and said hello to the attendants before walking to the bright cherry red sports car. He held the door open for me, and I slid into the sun-warmed leather. I caressed the supple, cream-colored leather and glanced around the car interior. "This seems familiar," I commented, more to myself than to Koa.

"It's the same car a certain television detective drove." The pride in his voice was clear.

"You're a fan?" I asked, suppressing a mock look of horror.

"Fan?" He shook his head as he pulled away from the curb. "No, not a fan. That's an insult. A possessive stalker would be more correct. Every day after school, I'd race home to watch the reruns. They were my babysitter. I can recite every line of every episode by heart."

My face twisted as I suppressed a smile. My babysitter had been a soap opera. We drove the twenty-mile-an-hour speed limit through the resort community to the main highway that would lead to the police department. Very normal to be in a high-performance sports car with the top down in Hawaii with a self-described stalker of a 1980s television show on the way to the police station to save my bestie from murder charges. Typical Tuesday.

Not far on the highway, we pulled off on the dirt shoulder in front of a colorful food truck. Koa jumped out and jogged around the car to hold the door open for me.

At the truck's window, Koa greeted the woman and ordered. A glance at the faded menu showed a small selection of breakfast sandwiches. We took seats to wait for our food at a metal picnic table off the side, watching the cars zoom by on the highway. Koa was busy on his phone while we waited, and I closed my eyes and enjoyed the sunshine. The food came out, steaming plates of saucy chicken with a salad and rice. One bite and I closed my eyes to enjoy all the flavors of savoriness. It hit the spot, as did the can of pomegranate-orange-grapefruit juice.

"So why are you helping us?" I asked between bites.

Koa chewed and stared out at the highway. I closed

my eyes and breathed in the freshness of the air and the heat of the sun on my skin, waiting for a response.

"I like you." Frank, honest, no pretense. I was thankful my sunglasses hid my shock. Rarely were people as honest as I thought I was. In all my years, I could count on one hand the amount of people that surprised me.

I nodded and took another bite so I couldn't say something embarrassing. Even if I wanted to, I wasn't sure what to say. My feelings for Koa exploded from vacation crush to straight-up full-blown something I didn't want to put a name on.

Thankfully, Koa changed the subject. "Have you been able to check on Zelda yet?"

"Yep, I checked on her at the hospital. All things equal, she's good. I think she was drugged."

Koa wiped his chin with a paper napkin. "What's your evidence of that?"

"She described feeling out of it after meeting Jeff, the victim, at the hotel lounge last night. Then blacking out."

"That is a possibility. Do you know if they ran any labs?

"From the discharge paperwork, they ran a full tox panel."

"Good, we'll need to request those records."

Enjoying the last of my meal, I smiled. "Are you an investigator?"

He threw back his head and chugged his juice. "Private investigator for the district attorney's office in San Diego. Retired. Now I help Sam on the few cases he catches."

I wanted to trust Koa. I really did. But trust was

something in short supply for me, and I had to question what organ or hormone I was thinking with. I wouldn't be handing it out to someone I just met, no matter how many butterflies they gave me. We threw our trash away and got back in the car. "Is everyone in your family in law enforcement?"

Koa punched the gas, and the sports car fishtailed onto the blacktop. "Sam's not, but he's the black sheep. Even my aunty worked dispatch for years in Hilo before she hurt her back."

We drove to the police station with the wind whipping my hair and my thoughts circling. My recent ex-boyfriend was the lead detective for the cops back home in Atherton. I appeared to have a type and wasn't sure how I felt about it. I pursed my lips at the thought of having butterflies for this man. At my age, I should have hot flashes, not the hots for a random man. Even if he was tan and had a thick head of curly hair that I wanted to run my fingers through.

The lobby of the sheriff's station looked little different from the one back home. I pushed down my anxiety and found a loose string at the hem of my T-shirt to play with. While Koa spoke to the desk officer, I took a seat in the waiting area. Was there a place for police stations to buy the same items all over the country? Like a catalog for law enforcement? I was lost in my thoughts of a police mail order catalog for uncomfortable chairs when a uniformed officer appeared in front of us.

"Hey man, is this our murderer's friend?" the buzzcut man inquired, hands on hips and a broad smile on his face.

Koa grimaced. "Not the best choice of words, bro." He stood and turned to me. "This is Lexi Burns, friend of Zelda Schultz. We just want to see her."

"Okay, man. Don't break her out, though. They should be done with the statement. Let me see where we are in the booking process."

I snorted.

Koa shook his head. "Again, not funny."

We followed the deputy down the hall when he suddenly turned back towards us. "Wait. Alexandra Burns?" he inquired, staring at me.

I nodded, my mouth dry and my palms wet.

He reached for my arm. "You're not seeing anyone until we get an official statement."

Koa moved to block him. "Hold on a minute. Lexi already gave a statement at the scene. Why is another statement being requested?" His tone was calm and official.

The deputy's jaw jutted out. "Hey, I don't care, man, but the sheriff said to get it so I'm getting it. In fact—" He leaned around Koa's shoulder. "Mike, Mike!" The guy at the front desk turned. "We got a warrant for an Alexandria Burns, don't we?"

Mike stared at the papers on the desk for a moment before holding up papers. "Yep, got it right here. Came down a few minutes ago."

"An arrest warrant? I called the crime in," I yelped, my voice rising in anger, my legs jelly. "Why is there a warrant?"

"Don't." Koa's stare silenced me. "Do not, Lexi, say another word." He turned to the deputy. "You can put us in a room, but we're not speaking until her attorney of record arrives."

The deputy shook his head. "Just gotta make things tough. We'll put her in a room, but you have to wait in the lobby. Or a bar somewhere." The flared nostrils said he was proud of the dig.

Koa smiled wider. "You thought things were tough before?" He pulled out his wallet and handed the man a card. "I'm an authorized paralegal for her attorney and have every right to be with her. And Zelda Schultz. We'll be representing both."

The deputy huffed. "Fine." He turned, and we followed down a dingy hall with thick, humid air. The smell of disinfectant and mold hung in the air. He deposited us in a room. "Not the best decision," he threw over his shoulder and slammed the door.

I dropped into the chair, my tailbone connecting with the metal under the flimsy cushion. "You're not an attorney, but a paralegal? Anything else? Cat burglar by night? Interpretative dance performer?"

Koa slid into the seat across from me. "Paralegal training was part of my job as an investigator, so I'm licensed. Sam established a practice here and I'm on the books, but it's for tax purposes. Strictly legal," he added.

I nodded, determined to get the full story soon.

"Sam is in with Zelda," he said. "They'll be done any time."

Right then the door opened, and Sheriff Martel, from the crime scene, walked in. His shirt wrinkled and his face drawn. "Miss Burns." He went to sit but stopped when he saw Koa was in the only other chair. Koa scooted out of the chair and stood at my side. "And you're her…" He glanced at a note on the cover of the manila file in his hand. "Legal representative?"

Koa nodded but remained silent. I swallowed hard. Was there a history between them? Could that work against Zelda and possibly myself? My fingers itched to reach for my phone and search for another attorney.

"Fine. Miss Burns, we have a few things we need to clarify." Martel cleared his throat and opened the folder, running his finger up and down the pages like he was looking for an answer. "Ah, how are you familiar with the victim?"

I shrugged, but Koa spoke before I could. "She's not answering questions. You have the statement. Anything you want clarification on can be through her attorney."

Martel clicked the pen and scratched notes. "When was the last time you saw Jeff Parks alive?"

"Hmpft." I leaned back and crossed my arms. I've watched enough mysteries to understand this guy was trying to get me riled up to say something he could run with, then use against me. No chance. "Next question," I replied in my kindest nurse voice.

"Did you have any arguments with the victim?"

I stared straight at him, lips pursed.

He leaned forward on the table, pen sat down. "It's a simple question."

"One she will not answer." Koa's tone allowed for no further discussion. I was glad to have him on my side.

The deputy huffed, made some notes, and closed the folder. "I'll have an officer type this up and get you to sign it."

"She's not signing anything right now. Send it to the office." Koa crossed his arms. "What about the arrest warrant?"

Martel feigned a look of shock. "What arrest warrant?" He glanced around the room at the empty air. "Did someone give you the impression there was one?" He shook his head, jowls jiggling. He bore a strong resemblance to a bulldog. "I'm real sorry about that. Just a misunderstanding."

"Are we done here?" Koa's tone could freeze the tropical ocean.

"We are."

"Then I can take my friend home?" I asked.

A genuine smile spread across his face. "Maybe."

With that, he left the room.

The door closed. Koa's and my eyes met. "That guy's about as reliable as a trained goldfish."

Chapter Six

"You know him?" I whispered as another deputy escorted us to where they held Zelda.

Koa barely nodded. "He's always been a try-hard. Always wanted to be more than he is."

The deputy opened a door. Zelda sat at a metal desk, her head resting on her folded arms. Sam faced her, one hand on the desk, the other on her back. She lifted her head when we entered. When our gazes met, her shoulders dropped. "Lexi!"

"Stand up," the deputy ordered.

Zelda threw him a side-eye that lacked her usual spunk. "You don't have to tell me twice."

She stood as he undid the cuffs bolting her to the table. Together, we followed the deputy out the door.

"Say nothing of consequence. The walls have ears." Koa whispered in my ear as we walked. The shiver that slid over my body wasn't just from the real danger we might be in.

I couldn't wait. "Are you okay, Zel?"

She shrugged. "I've been better, but also worse, so?" The smile that played at the edge of her mouth was the real Zelda. It was good to know she was in there somewhere. "Uh huh, this isn't a terrible place."

She glanced around the browned walls that might once have been white and the overhead fluorescent lights that glowed a dingy muddy yellow. "As far as police stations go, it's one of the nicer ones I've been in."

I stifled a laugh. I shouldn't be laughing. Someone was dead, but Zelda booked for murder and the entire situation was ridiculous.

Zelda glanced around at the lobby, as if she expected to be tazed any minute. "We're just walking out?"

"Yeah, I cleared everything before they let us in," Sam said as he brought up the rear of our group at a leisurely pace. "It's all good."

Koa held the door open while the deputy stared us down from the desk. "Don't mind him, he's still mad I stole his girlfriend twenty-five years ago."

The deputy's face soured further. "But I married her."

"And I thank you for your sacrifice, bro." Koa winked, and we slid out the front door of the police station.

I turned to Zelda halfway across the parking lot. "My God, Zel, what happened?"

She wiped a hand across her eyes, squinting at the sunlight. "They think I'm the murderer."

Koa's hands found our backs and maneuvered us towards a large SUV. "There are ears and eyes out here."

Understanding the warning, I didn't say anything else. I dug out an extra pair of sunglasses and handed them to Zelda before I slid my own on.

The headlights on an SUV parked in a handicapped spot blinked, signaling a remote unlocking. Sam opened the driver's side door. "Ladies." He hiked up his pants and extended his hand. "Get in, I'll give you a ride back to the resort."

"We were lucky to meet you," Zelda joked as she

eased into the back seat.

Sam hiked his ample butt into the driver's seat. "Luck has nothing to do with it. It's Honu looking out for you." Zelda stared. "The god of luck and mana? Spiritual energy?" Sam explained.

"That's for damn sure," Zelda said next to me. "I'll take all the gods' help."

Great, our attorney was aligned with her on a spiritual level. Let's hope he knew the law as well as he knew the pantheon of deities. I turned the conversation back to reality. "No bail?"

"Taken care of. It's all good if she stays on the island and makes herself available while we get this cleared up."

"Which I agreed to," Zelda chipped in.

I didn't think the police would let a murder suspect walk out of their custody without more effort. Did Sam have that much pull on the island? "Okay, but that seems odd, doesn't it? That they'd just let you go back to the resort?"

She shrugged. "Sorry, it's my first time being arrested for a felony. Not sure what the expectations are."

Sam scoffed with a head shake. "Eh, not that unusual. We're still on an island and while she might get to Maui or even Kaui, we're still thousands of miles from anywhere else. They'll be notified if she tries to fly out; they've put her on every airline watch list. And we can talk about the case specifics when we get you all back to the condo."

I let go of my reservations—for now. Zelda was right. All doubts and my late in life crush aside, Sam and Koa were good people who were willing to help us. We rode back to the resort in Sam's SUV, with Koa following in the sports car.

As promised, the front desk had a new condo assigned to us. After our things were released from the crime scene, the concierge had deposited them in the new room. We entered the new condo that, minus decor, was a replica of the previous room. This one featured a historical theme with antique maps of the area, colorful framed prints, and rich, dark wood accenting the light furniture and carpet.

Zelda and I dropped on the sofa as Koa opened the floor-to-ceiling sliders, letting a refreshing breeze in. Sam brought up the rear with two straining canvas tote bags.

"What's in the bags?" Zelda's interest peaked.

"Ah, Aunty wouldn't let me leave without packing some snacks." He gave a wink in our direction. "Got to keep the strength up."

"Sam…" Koa's tone held a teasing warning.

"So does Aunty know you're helping us?" Zelda asked, poking in the bags. Sam smacked her hand.

"She does. It takes someone spec—"

"Uncle." Koa's tone was a full threat. Sam's belly jiggled with laughter, and my cheeks reddened. "What's in the bag, again?" he asked, calmer.

Sam took a deep, dramatic breath, shaking his head. "Okay, I can take the hint. Good job changing the subject. Aunty packed all the good stuff.Musubi Spam, li hing candy, chips, and coconut candies." He laid them out on the table.

"Yes, please." Zelda tore into the chips as Sam pulled out a six-pack of beer. "Thank you."

Sam cracked a beer and handed it to Zelda before he

opened one for himself. "You're welcome, *kane*."

I took in Sam's untucked collared shirt and pants with a crease so sharp it could cut a tomato. Professional and relaxed. It inspired confidence, but it would take more than a good outfit to win me over. "I'm thankful, too, but have a few questions. I understand you're an attorney, our attorney now, Sam."

He nodded and folded liver-spotted hands on the table. "I am. Sam Iona, attorney at law. At your service."

"Have you handled mur—" I couldn't bring myself to say the word. "Cases like this before?"

"Yes, ma'am, I have. Have an outstanding track record too. Best in the islands, as a matter of fact."

"And you just happened to be Koa's relative? And just happened to be here?" The doubt was obvious in my words.

"Happened to be here, I live here." His face lit up. "I'm retired but help Ohana now and again, take the occasional case. Keeps me out of trouble. Koa's mom was my wife's sister." He directed his attention to Zelda. The humor was replaced with stone seriousness. "And lucky for you, I happen to be available, if I may say so." He cleared his throat, focused on Zelda. "Now tell me, ma'am, did you in fact kill Jeffrey Parks?"

Zelda paled. "No. No, I did not. I slept with him. That's all. I didn't know he was bad news until he stole the artifact."

Sam held up the beer bottle. "Hold up now. You just did the number one thing I tell all my clients never to do. The ones that follow my directions end up all right. The rest—" He held his palms up and shrugged. "Don't. That one thing is to only answer the question asked. Never volunteer information."

Zelda's mouth popped closed. My eyes widened. I could count on one hand the amount of people that had told her to shut up in her life, and few escaped without a pound of flesh missing.

"We're not great at that," Zelda admitted and shoved a handful of chips in her mouth. I chuckled. I wasn't sure if she was talking about us listening or keeping our mouths shut, but either way, she was right.

Sam ignored my laugh, dropped his hands back to the table, and took a swig of beer before he continued. "Good. You listen. We can work together. First thing, shut up. Then only answer questions after I say it's okay with a yes or no. Nothing more. Am I clear?"

Zelda leaned forward, resting her forearms on the table. She was taking this seriously. "Yes."

"I'm the one person who can get you out of this and I must know everything, and I mean everything. Now, you say you didn't kill this man, but you also didn't report finding the body. Is that correct?"

"I called," I interjected.

Sam's gaze shifted to me for a moment before settling back on Zelda. "How did he get in your bed?"

Zelda rubbed her forearms. "Not one hundred percent sure on that. I met up with him last night to talk about him stealing the artifact."

Sam's eyes widened. "Ah, I've been keeping an eye out for it." He patted his knee. "Wouldn't mind some of the effects of that myself. Let's keep that artifact avenue tabled for now. What happened when you met up with him?"

My hackles raised. Why would Sam be watching for the artifact? Surely he didn't believe in the myth of eternal youth—though could it be for the value of the artifact? These questions didn't help with my trust issues.

"We met at the hotel lounge, had a few drinks."

"How many is a few?"

"I think one?" Her head tilted. "I remember the bartender replaced the drink, but I don't remember that I finished the first one."

Koa had been leaning on the wall listening and took a seat at the table with us. "Uh-huh, did you get any of those cheese balls they serve down there? The ones with the goat cheese?" Zelda shook her head.

"You had a couple of drinks, nothing to eat," Sam continued. "What did you two talk about?"

"I told him he had to return the artifact, 'fess up, and I would go to the police first thing this morning."

Koa and Sam exchange a glance across the table. I grabbed a Misubi Spam and unwrapped the waxed paper.

"How did he react to that?" Sam questioned.

Zelda sat for a long time, and Sam repeated the question. Her eyes blinked rapidly. "I don't remember."

I leaned forward. "What do you mean?"

She cleared her throat and stammered. "I don't know what happened."

Koa reached across the table for Zelda's hand and took it in his. "It's okay. Tell us what you remember, even if it's just pieces or flashes."

Her shoulders relaxed, and she squeezed his hand. "I told Jeff to admit what he did. He kept rubbing my back and arm like that was going to get him anywhere." She rolled her eyes. "It was odd, like someone was dimming the lights in the lounge. I thought it was closing time and got up to leave. That's the last thing I remember." She inhaled, and I realized my breathing was shallow with anticipation. "Next thing I know, Jeff is dead next to me in bed."

"And here we are," Sam finished.

"Right." Zelda let out a nervous laugh. "Here we are."

Sam squeezed his hands together before dropping them to his lap and rubbing his thighs. "Sounds like you were drugged." He stood and turned to Koa. "You familiar with this bartender?"

Koa shook his head. "I don't spend much time in the lounge."

"The emergency room did a full drug panel," I interjected.

"Good, good. That will help." Sam threw back a handful of chips, stood, and paced around the small room. "How are you feeling now?"

"Okay? A little out of it, but how should I feel?"

"That aligns." Sam took another handful of chips before he continued. "What do you know about the artifact he stole?"

Zelda and I shook our heads. "Nothing besides what Koa mentioned on the tour."

Sam and Koa exchanged a glance I couldn't identify. Like Zelda and I, it appeared they could say much without a word between them.

"What do *you* know about the artifact?" I questioned. This was an opportunity for Koa and Sam to build trust with me and quench the doubt I couldn't shake.

Both men crossed their arms and gave small shakes of their heads. "Not much more than what's said on the tour," Sam said.

Goosebumps came out on my arms. Uh-huh, I would bet money both men knew more than they admitted to. What was there to hide? Would either of them benefit from the artifact or even Jeff's death?

"We're missing something big here, huge." Koa tapped his finger on the top of the beer can. I made a note of how quickly he changed the subject away from the artifact. "Something is going on that we're not seeing. Do you remember anything personal about Jeff?"

Zelda huffed. "You mean anything that I believed? Not a lot."

"There's a grain of truth in the lies somewhere, so tell us what you know."

"He said he lived in Seattle, worked in technology, and was here for a wedding."

"We should be able to verify all that easily enough. You never saw him with anyone?" Sam asked, between bites of Misubi Spam.

"Now that I think about it, no."

Growing silence filled the space with unasked questions and doubt. Zelda was hiding something. But what? In all our years, I could count the secrets I kept from her on one hand. How much had she kept from me? Since Koa and Sam clearly knew more than they were saying, why hide anything? Or was everyone hiding something?

We'd moved onto the balcony as the sun set over the ocean, a fresh breeze blowing. How could something be so beautiful and such a disaster at the same time?

Life never failed to knock me on my ass.

Sam pulled me out of my thoughts. "Now, here's a question I need answered. How do you two know each other?"

I sighed, relieved, the tension broken. Zelda regaled the men with antidotes of our forty-plus year friendship. The entire table burst out laughing more than once at our antics.

"No, no really. We weren't that drunk, and it's not our fault we misunderstood the German sign," Zelda went into exacting detail about when we drank our way through Oktoberfest, decided to explore an abandoned building and got stuck on a dilapidated staircase. Afraid we were going to be stuck for the night, we tied our coats and bags together into a makeshift ladder and made it out, but not without some scratches.

The laughter was wonderful medicine, along with the food. More than once, I caught Koa's stare on me and hoped he didn't notice the flush that spread over me. We were in the middle of a murder and a theft investigation. Now was not the time for cutesy, schoolgirl crushes.

The sun was setting when Sam left, reminding us not to leave the island, preferably the resort area, without his knowledge.

Zelda picked up the trash and wiped the table down before sighing and giving a yawn so fake no one with eyes would believe it. "Well, I've had an eventful day, going to hit the sack." She opened the bedroom door and peeked into the room. "No bodies, we're good. 'Night."

She closed the door, leaving Koa and me standing in the living room alone.

I struggled to inhale, my breath caught deep in my chest. "Koa, I—we—" I glanced at Zelda's closed door. "Appreciate your help."

His head dipped. "Don't give it another thought." Did I detect a blush rising on his tanned cheeks? "Sam and I have cut back our tours for the week. How about I take you to lunch tomorrow? Give you some time to sleep in?"

My head spun. "You're canceling work for us?"

Koa leaned into me, his warmth filled the space. "Sam and I are independent contractors. We do what we want, when we want. And right now, we want to help you."

Spurred on by his frankness, I asked, "Is this a date or a work meeting?"

A smile spread across his face. "A date. But I can bill you if it makes you happy? So it looks official."

A husky laugh escaped me. "I'm pretty sure that makes you a gigolo?"

He sauntered to the door. "I've been called many things, but that one is a first. See you at noon in the lobby?" I nodded. "Be hungry."

He left, and I closed the door behind him with a sigh. In one day, I had woken up to screams and a dead body, and had it end by being invited on a date by a man that gave my premenopausal heart butterflies. Not sure I could survive another day in paradise.

Chapter Seven

"Wait, you're going to lunch with him? Like a date? And you're wearing that?" Zelda asked, staring down at my outfit of terrycloth shorts and a T-shirt with a Nurse's Day logo across the front.

Self-conscious, I ran a hand over my usual ponytail. "What's wrong with this?"

She rolled her eyes. "Girl, I know it's been a minute since you went out with a new guy, and this is Hawaii and it's all casual and stuff—but you gotta step it up. You have a hot 'stache on the hook, reel him in."

"I don't understand half of what you just said, but if you think I should change, then say so."

Zelda grabbed my hand and dragged me into my bedroom. "Definitely changing. That man is hot and has the hots for you."

I rolled my eyes. "Don't forget a dead body was discovered in your bed just yesterday. Trivial things like men aren't that important right now."

She pulled the closet doors open and began inspecting items. "Yeah, well…I understand I didn't kill him, and I trust the universe to take care of me and the situation. And speak for yourself, men are always important…even if it's what got me in this situation."

Men were the trouble. I dropped on the bed and watched hangers fly across the rod as Zelda declined pieces. "Since when are you such a trusting soul?"

"Since the gods crossed our paths with Sam and Koa." She held up an olive-green maxi dress that featured a V-neck and a ruched waist.

We didn't have the same beliefs, and I rarely questioned hers, but I couldn't resist. "Okay, but then why did the gods let Jeff be murdered in your bed?" I didn't have the heart to tell her I wasn't convinced of their generosity. I appreciated it and accepted it but would keep my eyes one thousand percent open.

Zelda smiled and handed me the dress. "Because the gods are mysterious." She shrugged. "Or I do stupid stuff and they look out for me because I'm such a kind soul. Let's not question things too deeply, all right? Put this on."

I didn't put the dress on so much as Zelda pulled it over my head and smoothed it down my hips. "I still don't think now is the time for this."

She stood back to take me in. "Now is absolutely the time. There is no other time. I think half of our problems are because we're not living in the moment."

She turned her attention to the few pieces of costume jewelry I brought with me laid on top of the dresser. "None of this will work." She disappeared into her room and appeared with a gold necklace with a large brown and goldish stone dangling and a pair of gold hoops.

"Oh, no, Zel…this is too much for lunch," I tried to argue as she draped the necklace over my head. The stone nestled between my boobs.

"It's perfect. Tiger's eye is supposed to boost self-confidence and create harmony. So, you will be confident when you rip those tight little shorts off 'stache with harmony."

I laughed and agreed to the jewelry, not hoping she

was right but because the stone brought out the colors in my hazel eyes.

I left Zelda with strict instructions to stay away from men, read a book, and enjoy the leftover snacks from the previous evening, then deposited her on the beach before heading to the lobby to meet Koa for lunch.

In the stone drive, I found him leaning against the sports car. The tight shorts had been replaced with respectable khakis. The appreciative stares from tourists walking by weren't lost on me.

"You really took the week off?" I asked in a way of greeting. "Who's paying your bills while you're out lunching with the ladies?"

"The cost of living is high, but I manage." He shrugged. "I do what I want. It's always best to hit the case hard as early as possible." He held the door open, and I slid into the car. "You are beautiful," he whispered, throaty and deep, as he closed the door.

I slipped on sunglasses, but nothing could hide the thousand-watt smile that lit up my face as he took the driver's seat. "Thank you. Where did you retire from?" I changed the subject. No way was I going to let this Stache draw my focus away from the important things. Pretty sure.

Koa slid on sunglasses, waved at the valet, and eased the car out of the circle drive. "I put in my twenty years at the DA's office in Cali. Saved what money I could because I always wanted to come back to the island." The warm sun and cool breeze sent a pleasant shiver through me. Koa continued. "It's not all lying on the beach and surfing. That's why I do the tours. Helps offset the cost of living out and keeps me from dying of boredom, but not as exciting as a case."

Ah, and there was the secret. Zelda might believe Koa and Sam were sent from the Gods, but they were helping us because they missed the action of an investigation. "Until now?" I asked. His wink confirmed my suspicions.

Warmed by the sun, we drove with the top down, the radio turned to an oldies station, and no conversation. We pulled off the highway into a small dirt parking lot already packed with cars. Koa wedged between a couple trucks, and we walked into the one story, long wooden building.

We were seated on the back balcony overlooking the ocean and the rocky coast. He glanced at the menu before he sat it down. "What's your story?"

The server came, and we gave our orders, giving me a moment to decide whether to give him the abridged or unabridged version. A cheeseburger for me and a pulled pork sandwich with fries for him. We settled back into our seats after we ordered.

I stared out at the ocean before answering and exhaled hard. "Some stuff went down back home. Not awesome stuff. Zel and I wanted to get away for a while and decided Hawaii was the place to do it."

"Some stuff?" Koa inquired, sipping his water.

"Yeah, it was ugly, but we survived. We both quit our jobs." Koa's eyebrows shot up. "None of it was work-related. We'd both been in our careers for twenty years and decided we wanted a change." I sighed. "Kinda like you?"

His penetrating stare left me and traveled over the ocean scenery. "Life-altering events have a way of making you see things differently."

I wondered if there was such an event in his past but

couldn't ask. The last thing I wanted was to trauma bond with a hunk. I huffed a laugh. "That's for damn sure." I rubbed my bare arms, self-conscious of the fading scars. "Yeah, so that's my story."

He leaned his elbows on the table, his gaze penetrating through me. "You came to paradise to heal."

"And now, we're mixed up in a murder." I shrugged. "So much for relaxing."

"If there's one thing I've learned, Lexi, you can't run from the past. Whatever it is, it'll always catch up to you." He leaned forward. "And it usually bites you in the ass. If you don't mind me being frank."

I threw him a glance that was known to wither the most uppity physician. "Those events are too fresh, and I don't take well to being told what to do. While I appreciate frankness, you don't know what I experienced, or what Zelda went through. Please don't make assumptions." I added the "please" to soften things.

His jaw worked and he stared at the worn table before meeting my gaze. "Noted, sorry if I crossed a line."

My eyebrow arched and my mouth opened, but the server brought our plates, and I was grateful for the interruption. An apology in under a minute? I took the moment to gather myself. "I must face what happened, but now is not the time. Getting Zelda out of trouble is my focus right now."

Koa smiled. "Why do I feel like that is sometimes a full-time job?" He took a bite of his sandwich while I told him stories about Zel and me. Mostly of her getting into trouble and me getting her out of it.

We ate and shared about our lives, his time in

California and mine in Atherton, Missouri. Surprisingly, we had much in common. Time slipped away fast, and I realized I enjoyed myself. Guilt rose in me for how much. I pushed my empty plate aside and pulled a notebook out of my tote. There were some things I wouldn't be sharing with Koa or Sam, regardless of what they counseled. Not until I trusted them fully.

"I have so many questions about Jeff and who he was. Should we do a background check? You can do those online for, like, forty bucks, right?"

Koa shook his head, setting his napkin aside. "Unnecessary. We should have most of his personal information in the sheriff reports."

"Okay, great, I'll let you handle that." My charge nurse hat was on, and Koa suppressed a smile. "There's more to Jeff than a simple tech bro on the island for a wedding." My head spun with all the questions running through it. "Something about that artifact is bothering me...why steal it on a tour? Why wasn't it more obvious someone on the tour took it?"

"That leads me to believe Jeff was really a tech bro. The security was overrun." Koa smiled. "The museum might look like it has little or no security, but it's high tech all the way."

"Cameras?" My excitement perked. It's possible the cameras caught someone or something else.

"Nothing that mundane. Infrared scans and sensors that are so sensitive they can tell how many people are in a room from their breath."

My brows furrowed. "Zelda mentioned Jeff had some foil-looking stuff with him in the museum, do you think that's how he got it out?"

"My guess is the material disrupted the system, and

by the time security figured it out, he was out with it. That would explain why, with all their technology, they couldn't detect how the artifact left the building."

"It was a shield of sorts." I scribbled furiously in the notebook. The artifact was the key. "He was able to hide in plain sight on the tour. Who would use a tour bus as a getaway vehicle?"

"Agreed." The server came and cleared the table. Koa ordered a dessert with coffee.

The server returned and placed a tall dessert dripping in chocolate sauce, surrounded by macadamia nuts and whipped cream. "First, Hulu Pie. A specialty of the islands."

He handed me a spoon, and I dived in, stifling a moan when the combination of ice cream and chocolate flooded my mouth. "Oh, I could eat this all day," I groaned around a mouthful of lusciousness.

Koa smiled. "I've put on ten pounds since I moved back. I blame Aunty's cooking, but it's this stuff." He dipped his spoon in, pulling another huge bite. I wondered where those ten pounds were on him, self-conscious of all extra ten and then some of mine.

We scraped the plate clean and set the spoons down, my stomach full.

"We need to make a stop." Koa stood. "Case related."

We drove down the highway, through the interior of the island. The land changed from black lava flow to deep green rolling hills. Farms dotted the roadside, and the air cooled slightly. I leaned my head back and closed my eyes, enjoying the warm sun and cool breeze on my skin. The music complemented, instead of fighting with, the wind whipping around the car's interior. We turned off the paved road onto a dirt road, flat and well maintained. Greenery enclosed both sides of the road, creating a canopy.

The butterflies returned to my stomach. In other circumstances, this would be a romantic, peaceful drive. I trusted Koa enough to get through this, and I wouldn't let myself go any further…yet. My foot kicked my tote on the floorboard. It was hefty enough if he did anything shady, I could swing hard enough to cause some damage.

The tunnel opened to a clearing with a rambling clapboard house with a wraparound porch. Koa parked out front and hurried around to let me out. The front yard was littered with toys and an occasional chicken running through it. He led me up the front steps and knocked on the screen door before throwing it open and walking inside. I followed.

"Mikala," Koa hollered through the house. "You home, Hoa?" We stood in an area living room. Chairs and couches littered the room, making it feel cozy without feeling crowded. The walls featured family photos, from sepia to black and white to color.

A woman's voice yelled from the hall halfway down the building. Koa followed the sound down the hall, passing through the kitchen and the living room. The second door was ajar. He pushed it open and stepped inside.

The room was all white and Scandinavian furniture. Bright and airy. A desk sat against the wall. and a woman sat in an ergonomic chair with her back to us. Her hair was pulled back in a long black ponytail that cascaded to the seat.

"Hey, Koa, you bring me something?" she said over her shoulder, not turning around from the computer.

He held out the bag full of hot, greasy malasadas. She took it without looking, opened it, and took a bite of one. She moaned and closed her eyes before shoving the whole thing in her mouth. She chewed, wiped her hands on her legs, and opened her eyes to stare at me.

"What? You've never seen a woman enjoying a pastry?" she asked.

I shook my head and smiled. "Far from it. I'm appreciating a likeminded woman. Few things in this life are as enjoyable as a good pastry."

She stared at me a moment longer before holding the bag out to me. I had already had my fill but couldn't back out now. Taking one out of the bag, I took a huge bite, the filling spilling on my hand, and I licked it off with a smile.

"My girl," she said appreciatively. She glanced at Koa. "Finally, you bring a good one around. Took you long enough."

"Stop it." He dropped down in a nearby chair. "What do you have?"

She handed me a napkin before turning back to the computer. Picking up a file, she turned back to us. "First of all, I'm Mikala." She threw a side eye at Koa. "My cousin here didn't properly introduce us."

"Nice to meet you, I'm Lexi." I gave her a little wave and took a seat near Koa.

He waved his hand in a hurry up motion. "Back to what you found."

"Calm your tits, bro. Where do you have to be?" She rolled her eyes. I stifled a laugh, and she continued. "First, your friend? He is not what he appeared to be."

"I had a hunch."

"Mr. Park's annual income, as reported on his tax

returns, falls in the neighborhood of $70K."

"Respectable," I said and threw a knowing glance at Koa. "And not surprising."

"Yes, solidly middle class. But that doesn't account for Jeff's gambling habits." Mikala pulled a sheet of paper out and handed it to me. I held it for Koa to read and he leaned closer. Jeff had been spending on average $10,000 a month on credit cards and paying them off each month.

I held the paper out to her. "This is impossible on his income."

She nodded. "Even more interesting is that $20,000 was recently deposited into his account. Except for the past four months, zero dollars went in, but the regular $10,000 went out."

Jeff had been racking up gambling debt at an alarming rate. "It would take him decades to pay this back."

Koa and Mikala nodded. He said, "Something another contact of mine found was thousands of calls to a burner phone on the mainland."

"Any texts?" she asked at the same time I opened my mouth.

Koa smiled. "A couple. Cryptic at best." He took paper out of the front pocket of his shirt and unfolded it before handing it to Mikala.

She took it and glanced over it. "Hmmm .... this looks like code. Def cryptic."

I held my hand out and she passed the paper my way. The messages were about the weather, and then changed to moonlight without any clear transition. I studied them, and it hit me. "The sun is the volcano, Mauna Loa. The moonlight is the museum. They are giving him directions on how to steal the artifact."

Koa's eyebrow rose. "Jeff had a partner? Was it Zelda?"

I clicked my tongue. The fact he would even ask about Zel raised my blood pressure.

"Two people could be working together, but that doesn't feel right," Mikala suggested. "This feels like the dude is out here doing his own thing."

"Zelda was a distraction in this whole thing. Everything about their relationship was a distraction." I said, now more insistent. "Jeff was after something bigger, something worth more."

Koa leaned back. "You think he stole the artifact to pay off his debts, and Zelda was a decoy to distract?"

Mikala leaned back in her seat and stretched her arms over her head, crossing her hands behind her head. Silence spread through the room. My thoughts traveled back to the day of the bus tour.

"That's it! He tried to get rid of it when we stopped at the beach, but something happened, it didn't work out."

A smile spread over Koa's face. "So, then he met up with the buyers at the resort and things went south."

Deep in thought, I tapped my fingers on my lips. "The question is, how did he find out how to get rid of an item on the black market, and did he have a buyer already set up?"

Mikala laughed. "Easy, I'll do a deep dive into his activities."

A sudden exhaustion washed over me, and I yawned.

"How about we get you back to your room for a nap?" Koa suggested. "You can relax for a while, while we do some digging on Jeff." He stood, the decision made. "Mik, thanks for your help, and be careful." She waved him away, already focused on the task. "Mik?" His tone was now a warning.

"Yeah, yeah," she said absently and waved again. "I'll be careful."

I stood and smoothed down my dress. "Thanks again, Mikala." She didn't glance my way as we made our way out of the house and into the car.

The door barely closed when I turned to Koa. "Hold on, I'm an adult and can do stuff." My words sounded childish even to my ears.

He leaned back and shifted the car into gear. "I recognize that. But I also recognize you need rest, you're exhausted. I'm not patronizing you, Lexi. But you're no good to Zelda if you're out of it."

Guilt rose in me, and I averted my gaze. Koa picked up on in. "Do you want to help Zelda?" he asked, his voice low.

I rubbed my hands together and then across my forehead. My thoughts and emotions were a whirlpool. I might have doubts about Zelda, but those words would never cross my lips, and I was ready to fight someone that said so. Especially to a man I barely knew and didn't trust one hundred percent.

"Zelda is a part of me." My tone ended the topic. "Let's head back. I could use that nap."

We drove back to the resort, my eyes drooping. It seemed like every day I discovered another level of relaxation I didn't understand. Or was it exhaustion?

As we crossed the lobby, a cool breeze ruffled my hair and sent the scent of Koa's aftershave my way. My mind wandered into devilish thoughts, and I walked slightly behind him, better to take in the view of the beach as well as his backside and wide shoulders. I wouldn't act on it, but I could enjoy it a little.

A piercing scream shattered my dirty thoughts. "Alexandra!"

I stumbled over my feet before coming to a stop, the maxi dress tangling around my legs. "Mom?"

Chapter Eight

My mother bolted toward me; engulfing me in a flurry of fabric and frizzy curls. "My bubala!"

She squeezed me and I tried to return the hug, knowing it would never be as rib-crushing as hers. My eyes threatened to pop out of my skull. A groan escaped me as we separated.

"Hal, come here. I found her," Mom shouted over her shoulder. All heads within earshot turned, and my cheeks flushed.

I ducked my head. "Mom, I think everyone knows you found me."

Her arms rested on mine and she gave me a shake. "After everything you've been through, seeing you again is like water for a desert flower."

"Mom…" I started again as she pulled me into another bone-crushing hug.

Over her shoulder my dad shuffled over. "Lexi, you're looking good, girl!" My mom released me long enough for my dad to get a quick hug and kiss in. "We've got a room in the south tower. Is that close to you and Zel?"

"No, gosh, no. We're in the west tower." For the blessing of no adjoining rooms, I would say a prayer to all of Zelda's goddesses.

"Well, guess we'll go on home then," he said with a

71

laugh.

I joined in. His dad jokes were ancient, but also the best.

Koa cleared his throat behind me, drawing my parents' attention. I turned to see a wide smile under the mustache.

"Well, well, who is this, Alexandra?" My mother's tone told me she'd taken in his thick hair and muscular build and approved.

"Mom, Dad, this is Koa." I paused for a beat to summarize the last few days since we hadn't yet told them about Zelda's situation. "A friend." Keep it simple, I warned myself. "Koa, these are my parents, Harold and Ruth Burns."

Koa held out his hand to my mother. "Pleased to meet you, ma'am. Sir."

My dad's opinion of people was based more on handshakes than physical appearances. When the two men shook hands, I noted the approval in my father's eyes. "Any friend of Lexi's is a friend of ours."

Drool ran from my mom's mouth. "Absolutely." I elbowed her.

"Lexi and I were coming back from lunch. I'm just escorting her back to her room," Koa said in his tour guide voice.

"Ohhhh, a gentleman." My dad turned to stare at my mom's inflection.

"Yeah, he's going to escort me to the room. How about you give me a minute to change, find Zelda, and we meet by the pool? Or the beach?"

My mom's stare was still on Koa, but my dad answered. "No can do, pumpkin. We've got dinner plans with a guy we met. Not as nice as this young man." He gestured to Koa. "But he has a farm and invited us to his place. We'll catch up at breakfast." He leaned over and kissed my cheek before he pulled my mom back to the wicker chairs overlooking the grounds. My mom threw a wiggly wave over her shoulder. I was confident it was for Koa.

I inhaled and exhaled hard before heading down the hall. Next to me, Koa chuckled. "And I thought Zelda was a lot."

I smiled. "They weren't like this when I was growing up. This is all since they retired."

Koa's laugh made me shiver. He spoke softly and rested a hand on my back as we walked down the hall. "I'm doing something wrong in retirement then. You seemed to forget to tell them something important."

"I didn't forget. I'll tell them when I'm ready."

He nodded and dropped his hand. We said goodbye as the elevator door opened. I hopped in with a wave and a sigh of relief. My attraction was growing, but so was my suspicion. On the surface Koa was great, but there was more there.

But was it nefarious?

In the elevator, I had to remind myself of Koa's point that I had to be well to help Zelda. I didn't bother taking off my clothes, kicked my sandals to the side and fell on the bed, and pulled a throw blanket over me.

The sun was low in the sky, the room in shadows, when the door jiggled open. Groggily, I pushed myself up and shook the sleep from my brain.

"Lexi?" Zelda's voice traveled through the sitting room to the bedroom. "Lex, you here?"

"Yeah," I answered and ran my hands through my hair which was now a cause lost to sea salt and humidity.

"Just a second." I adjusted my clothes and blew out a big breath.

I walked out of the bedroom when Zelda hit me with a full body contact hug. A glance over her shoulder showed Sam closing the front door of the condo. I let out a groan and wrapped my arms around her. So many hugs today.

"I left you," I whispered in her hair as the weight of recent events hit me.

"Shhhh…you missed nothing." Zelda pulled back and kissed my cheek. "I'm fine. Lucky for me I have the best attorney in the islands and probably most of the western mainland. And I got a text from your parents that they're here."

"We ran into them in the lobby on the way back from lunch. You've been following the rules?" I asked.

Zelda released me and nodded. "Yep, one hundred percent, heart and soul."

I gave Zelda another big hug, and didn't let her go for a long time. Until I knew for sure the tears had passed. She meant everything to me.

We settled on the balcony with diet sodas and a bag of carry out that magically appeared. "Sam recommended this place on the delivery app." She sat the bag on the table and unpacked the containers. I didn't think I was hungry again, but the scent of grilled meats wafted to me. Zelda grabbed a fork and dug in a container of fries drenched in steak, shrimp, and a sauce that smelled divine.

I let out a low whistle and tried to make a joke out of it. "You promise on your heart and soul? That serious?"

Zelda smiled around a mouthful of fries and meat.

"It is. My ass is in a sling, Lex." The smile dropped. "I'm more than concerned how I'm going to get out of this." Her fork picked at the food. "But I have faith I will get out of it." She gave me a weak smile. "I have to."

I sat quietly, trying to figure out what to say. I caught her up on the afternoon with Koa.

"Curious. So, you two have something in common?" Zelda asked, setting her food aside.

I nodded and felt the warmth flood through me. Possibly I could handle a fling and get Zelda out of trouble. But I felt Koa was more than a fling, and getting Zelda out of this might be one for the record books. "Did Sam say the sheriff had anything new? Have they found a weapon yet?"

She placed the container down and crossed her hands over her stomach, tucking her chin and blowing out a big breath, looking for all the world like an old lady about ready to drop a bomb.

"Not yet. The only actual piece of evidence is the witness."

Chapter Nine

"What?" The rice container slid from my hand to the floor. I sat on the edge of my seat in indignation, ready to throw punches at whoever would spread such lies. "No way in hell someone saw you do it!"

"All we know is it's a male, mid-twenties, local. Sam said the witness gave an excellent description of me." Zelda shrugged and the corners of her lips turned up in a "I told you so" expression. "Sam said eyewitness accounts are all but trash though."

I huffed. "Isn't that the truth? We know firsthand exactly how messed up eyewitnesses can be."

Her eyes widened, and her gaze never blinked. "The police didn't have a choice but to arrest me to keep me on the island until they sorted things out and make sure I didn't leave before, but now with the witness coming forward…" She drew up her right leg and laid it on the table. "I get to wear this snazzy accessory."

I squirted at the thick black thing encircling her ankle. "Is that…?" I asked, trying to process what she held in front of me.

"Yep, an ankle bracelet. Supposedly waterproof so as not to ruin my vacation." A strained laugh escaped her. Her chest rose and fell fast in short breaths. "It doesn't exactly go with my swimsuit wardrobe but definitely gives me an air of mystery, doesn't it?"

I held up my hands. "Wait, wait, Zel. Go back to the

witness. Legit, that's all you know? The body in your bed was enough; now there's a witness, too?"

Zelda nodded. "Sam said the police can't possibly be looking at me as a serious suspect." She kicked her leg up in the air again and wiggled her toes.

My brows constricted. "But the sheriff is looking at you as a serious subject, or you wouldn't be wearing that thing."

Zelda reached for a can of juice and pulled her hand away. "Sam says not to worry."

"Funny how things keep piling up." My lips pursed. Sam's advice didn't make sense. "You can leave the resort with that thing on?"

"Yes, I could probably go surfing with it on and be fine."

I rolled my eyes. "Let's not ensure your death. You just learned to swim last year."

"I'm at least getting in the ocean and splashing around."

I nodded and leaned back, but I didn't understand enough about getting arrested and charged with murder to know what was wrong with what Zelda said, but her fake confidence didn't fool me. Could this all be bravado to cover her guilt, or real fear for the seriousness of the situation?

"Where's the paperwork they gave you when the sheriff released you?"

Her face was a smooth mask. "I didn't get any. Maybe they gave it to Sam?"

Goosebumps broke out on my arms. I'd lost count of the times Zelda had been arrested back home for protests or demonstrations. This wasn't her first time around the park. "Don't they usually give you something? Like a discharge slip? Didn't you sign something?"

"I didn't sign anything. I figured Sam took care of everything." Zelda's eyebrows scrunched together. "Which seems odd in hindsight, doesn't it? I'll think about it in the morning. When my head is clear."

"No, Zelda." Her eyebrows raised at the severity of my tone. "Something isn't adding up. The police took the eyewitness account seriously enough to put an ankle bracelet on you. And while I appreciate Koa and Sam's help...yeah...something doesn't add up there either." I rubbed a hand across my face. "It's a bit much for two women neither man had met until a few days ago." I shook my head. "Zel, I understand you want to put all your faith in the goddess or whatever. I'm scared. Of what could happen, and what you're not telling me." I left the rest unsaid, and it hung in the air between us.

Zelda cleared her throat and stood, wiping her hands down her denim shorts. "I'm going to bed. I'll see you in the morning." She turned and headed into her room.

"Zel, don't. I didn't mean to hurt your feelings or whatever, but you know how you are."

She turned on her heel and was at my side in a heartbeat. Fire in her features and ice in her words. "And how am I, Lex? Please explain, because clearly after forty-three years I don't understand myself."

Zelda and I were as different as night and day, but our friendship ran deeper than blood. I may have overstepped, but this wasn't a simple arrest for a political protest or one of our shenanigans. This was life or death. "Something is wrong here, and I don't want you to end up the scapegoat. I want you to keep an eye open. We both need to keep our eyes open. You're not stupid, but you tend to not make the best decisions." The words may have been true, but as soon as they left my mouth, I regretted them.

"But"—she spat the word out—"you know what that word means, don't you? Everything before it doesn't matter. You really mean exactly what you just said."

My heart fluttered, and my stomach twisted. "Zelda." My tone took on the edge I reserved for noncompliant patients. "I don't want to lose you."

"Right, because then how else would you feel superior?" Zelda stalked to her bedroom. No door slammed and no screaming. The silence was painful enough.

****

The next morning, the tension was thicker than molasses in winter. I waited patiently for Zelda to appear in the living room, my stomach grumbling. Another text from my parents showed they would be late for breakfast and might miss us. At the rate Zelda moved, they probably wouldn't.

When she finally did appear, she wouldn't meet my gaze and the elevator ride to the lobby restaurant was silent. The distance between us bigger than the island.

We ordered and waited, our attention everywhere but on each other until the drinks came. "Are we going to talk about last night?" Zelda asked, squinting hard at the lush landscaping.

As I swallowed, the juice burned the back of my throat. As far as I was concerned, it was all on her. We'd been friends long enough for me to recognize that route would not work here.

"Zel, I didn't mean you make poor decisions. I have little room to talk." I let out a dry laugh. "You trust people more than you should sometimes, but that's what makes you who you are, and awesome." I shrugged. "I wouldn't change that about you."

She met my gaze for the first time since last night. "You might be right. And thanks." She sipped her morning mimosa. "But come up with a better way of saying it next time?"

My throat relaxed, and I sighed with relief. "Understood."

Zelda dug into her food, quiet again. "I understand not putting all our trust in one thing or person."

"Like the goddess?" I went out on a limb with the joke and got rewarded immediately with a mischievous grin.

"Exactly. Why pray to one when there is a pantheon available? We're smart women; let's figure this mess out."

She stared at the luscious green lawn dotted with exotic, colorful flowers. "Lexi." She cleared her throat and made a small noise, holding back tears. "We have a lot in life, really, we do. But the thing I value most and couldn't live without is you." She dropped my hand, wiped hers across her eyes, and sniffed. "I would never lie to you. Ever. You have to trust that."

I swallowed the lump in my throat. She might not lie, but conveniently forgot details. At what cost to both of us? I nodded, "We can do this." I held her hand in mine. "I must trust you." There was no other option.

The conversation was cut short by the arrival of my parents. Neither Zelda nor I had told them about the murder, and it had to be done sooner rather than later. Hugs and compliments were exchanged, and everyone took their seats as the server brought fresh drinks.

They ordered breakfast, and my dad regaled the server with a flurry of dad jokes. She finally escaped, and he continued, "Oh man, girls, you should have come with us last night. This guy's house, well, really a compound." My mom nodded her head. "Amazing. Dinner sourced all fresh from his land."

"Next time, he said we'll go out on his boat. You girls will have to come with us. Catch us up on everything." Mom leaned her elbows on the table and glanced between Zelda and I expectantly. "Especially the gentlemen." She wiggled her eyebrows. Zelda coughed and reached for her drink, motioning me to speak. Her face still blotchy.

I took a deep breath and dived in. "The men will have to wait."

My mom frowned. "Oh, no. Not that sexy mustachioed one? If I was thirty years younger…"

"And single," Dad added, absently scrolling on his phone. "Seeing if I can find the photos of these mashed potatoes from last night. They were purple, if you can believe that."

I rolled my eyes. "Especially that one. We've got a situation on our hands." I took a deep breath and dove in. "A body was found in Zelda's bed a few days ago, and she's being investigated for the murder." I paused for a count to ten to let my words sink in. "Koa was a private investigator when he lived and worked on the mainland. Now that he's living here on the islands, he and his uncle Sam, an attorney, are helping us out."

My parents stared at us, open-mouthed.

"But I only slept with him," Zelda said proudly. "I didn't murder him."

I grimaced internally.

Dad waved a hand as he picked up a muffin. "Zelda, honey. We've known since you were in eighth grade you were…shall we say…free with your affections?"

Mom nodded. "Sorry, who did you sleep with, dear? The sexy mustache?"

"Definitely not, Lexi has dibs on that one," Zelda emphasized. "Jeff is the dead guy. But I didn't murder him. I want that clear. At least, I think I didn't."

Dad tore the paper lining off the muffin and took a bite. "Of course you didn't, sweetheart. You might be a lot of things, Zelda, but not a murderer."

Zelda's eyes watered. "Thanks."

Mom nodded with a smile. "That's a relief." She leaned back and stretched. "So, you've got some locals helping you out? Do you need our help?"

Zelda and I answered together with a strong "No."

I continued. "I'll get Zelda out of this." I reached for Zelda's hand and squeezed. "We will."

"Good." Dad waved a hand. "You two together can take on anything. Now, let me tell you about these mashed potatoes this guy served last night. Whoa." The topic was done and now on to food.

Mom reached for my hand and squeezed it. "And you're healthy again, Alexandra. We're happy to see that, and you don't need us bugging you."

The server brought their breakfast, and I was surprised how easy it was for them to accept everything. Listening to Dad talk about the potatoes, I kind of understood how easy the situation was to forget in comparison to the glorious spuds.

We finished breakfast, made plans with my parents to meet up every day for breakfast, headed back to the room to change, and went straight to the beach. The sun didn't feel as bright as it did yesterday, but it was beautiful just the same. We floated in the ocean and sunned ourselves before I pulled the notebook back out and dug a pen from the bottom of my tote.

"Okay, I'm going to write down what we know and go from there."

Zelda leaned back in the chair and closed her eyes. "We met at the pool one evening. They played the song by that Swedish band from the eighties, the one about that dangerous girl? He started singing with me." A smile spread across her face. "Then, things just happened."

"At the pool?" I didn't bother to hide the contempt in my voice. "Like where kids play?"

Zelda opened one eye and stared at me. "It's not like we did it with kids there. It was dark, and no one was around."

I rolled my eyes. "That you saw." And made a note of it. They may have been seen, either by the supposed witness or someone else with an interest in the situation. I put a large question mark in the margin. "How many times did you two hook up?"

"Three times? Once by the pool and twice in the gardens by the golf course." A sly smile spread across her face. I envied Zelda and her free ways, even when they led her to serious trouble. "You had no idea what he was up to until we arrived at the museum?"

She shook her head. "No idea. He seemed normal. Even at the museum, he seemed hyper but not weird. Not that I have experience with thieves."

I sat the notebook aside and dug a bag of snack mix out of my tote. "Then the beach…what happened there? You said you thought you heard voices?"

"Yeah, but not screaming and fighting. More tense,

you know? Low voices, I heard hissing, but it could have been the cat."

"Did you actually see the cat?"

Zelda's eyebrows scrunched. "Now that you mention it, no, I didn't. When I got close, there was a bunch of movement. Jeff saw me and yelled, and I ran. He was close on my heels."

"So, there might not have been a cat?" I asked. "That would explain his desire to push me away when I cleaned his wounds. He didn't want me to see what they were." I thought back to that day. What did the wounds look like? I silently cursed myself for being distracted by Koa and everything else. If I paid more attention that day, we'd have had more answers.

She shook her head. "If it wasn't a cat, what could it have been?"

"A person, someone he was meeting, but let's put it on the list to go back and look at those woods. I'm down for exploring another beach."

I wrote "*beach – cat?*" in the notebook. "Was there anyone from the hotel lounge you recognized? Did you feel anyone watching you?"

She shook her head. "I have no idea. Everything after I sat down is a blur."

I tapped the pen on the notebook and drew an enormous question mark. Was it a coincidence that Zelda didn't see or remember much? Convenient forgetfulness or drugs? I pushed the thought away. It didn't matter which it might be, I must trust Zelda. Those were questions I had to stop.

"Someone was aware you were meeting him and set you up."

Zelda raised her arms and crossed them at the wrists

above her head, like she didn't have a care in the world. "Jeff said he used to come here all the time. As much as I hate to admit it, I'm probably not the only woman he's fooled around with on the island."

"I agree. No offense."

"None taken. I wouldn't be surprised." She exhaled hard. "I think he stole the artifact because of the gambling debt. Koa said it was worth a lot."

"It's possible." I made another note to follow up with Koa on the background. Something occurred to me. "Are you sure he said he used to come here?"

"Yeah, why?"

"I'm wondering if it was when he was a kid. With his family?"

"I don't think so. When I mentioned my mom had passed a couple of years ago, he got weird and said his dad was an ass."

My intuition perked up. "That's all?" Zelda nodded. "I understand you—" I was interrupted by my cell phone dinging a text notification.

Koa wrote —*I've got some information for you. When can we meet?*—

I responded —*We're free whenever. Are you on a tour?*—

He answered – *I'm doing some business. Should be back at the hotel by four or so.*—

Me –*Let's meet in the lounge and chat.*—

Him –*Sounds good. Whatever you do in the meantime, do not talk to the police. I cannot stress this enough.*—

I gave his comment a thumbs-up emoji, then laughed and handed the phone to Zelda. She rolled her eyes. "Like I need to be told that one, but okay," she said sarcastically. "Sam was very clear on that yesterday. You know, as an educator with twenty years of experience, I'm offended that people don't think I can follow simple directions. Also, I'm curious exactly what type of business Mr. Stache is taking care of."

"Uh huh." I bit my tongue to avoid saying something I'd regret. I put away my notebook, and we took another dip in the ocean. This time, the water slipped over my skin and calmed my aching muscles. My body was invigorated when we walked out of the water, breathing heavily and relaxed.

Here, next to our loungers, wearing the khaki uniform, stood the sheriff with a gun on his hip. We slowed our steps.

"Well, shit," Zelda said with finality.

Chapter Ten

"Remember, don't say anything," I whispered to Zelda as we crossed the sand. I plastered a smile on my face. "Sheriff, what can we help you with today?"

His return smile was ice. "Zelda Schultz?" His stare darted between us before it settled on Zelda.

"The one and only." My words were strong.

"We met yesterday at the police station. I'm Mike Martel. I interviewed you." He held out a hand to her.

I blocked his hand. "With her attorney." I kept my voice measured. "Whom, we note, is not present now. So why are you?"

His smile fell. "I just had a few more questions. Nothing you need an attorney for, I assure you."

I stepped in front of Zelda. "You're not speaking to her unless her attorney is present, and certainly not on a beach."

"Ma'am..." he said, his voice sounding tired. "I'm not here about the homicide. I have questions about the artifact that Jeff stole."

My hackles rose. He knew more than he had let on. How much more did he know? "What about the artifact?"

"I have reason to believe you and your friend here know where it's at. We just want to know where it is."

"Do you have a warrant to search her things, or are you here to arrest her? Again." Zelda grasped my arm, whether in fear of her seeing the inside of a jail again or my mouth, I wasn't sure.

"I don't, but if we could just chat…"

"Nope, not happening." I waved a hand in dismissal. "Scoot."

Martel's head tilted and his gaze laser focused on me.

My chin lifted and I waved again. "Go on, scoot."

He shook his head. "If that's how you want to play, fine. It will only make things harder." He turned and trudged a path across the sand.

We watched as he crossed the lush green lawn. Before he disappeared into the resort, he met up with the security director. We watched as they walked away in conversation. I stepped away from Zelda and exhaled. "What the hell was that?"

Zelda shook her head. "I don't know, but I don't like it."

"Agreed. Let's go back to the room, and you call Sam. Tell him what happened."

We gathered our things up and dragged them inside. "You know, I was ready to answer those questions, thinking I was helpful." She shook her head. "I guess I need to hear something a few times for it to sink in."

I wrapped an arm around her as we waited for the elevator. "I know, Zel. That's what I love about you. You have the biggest heart and—"

"The biggest mouth," Zelda finished as she laughed and entered the elevator.

Upstairs in the room, we went to our separate rooms, showered, and dressed before meeting in the living room. Zelda brought her phone in and had already missed calls from Sam. She listened to the voicemails, her face scrunched, before her eyes widened and finally her face reddened from embarrassment.

"Oh no, Lex." Zelda shook her head. "Here you were worried about me."

I grabbed a wine cooler from the fridge and a bag of chips and dropped on the couch next to her. "I haven't done anything." She gave me a side eye. "Literally, except for sleeping and eating. That's pretty much it."

Her eyebrow raised. "Apparently, you have ticked off one Sheriff Martel. He reached out personally to Sam. Said if you don't stay out of his way, he's going to charge you with obstruction of justice."

"Ugh, men." I groaned and sipped the wine cooler. "I know that's a thing but telling him to scoot isn't obstruction. Annoyance of justice, maybe?" I shoved a handful of chips in my mouth. "Wow, the sheriff called Sam just to complain about me. Nice. I feel special."

"I'm going to try to call Sam." Zelda dialed the number, and we waited while it rang.

"Aloha, Sam here."

"Hey, it's Zelda. You're on speaker. What's going on?"

A heavy sigh carried across the line. I stared at the phone with indignation. Why, when a woman stood up for herself, it usually ended badly—or at least with heated words. "I got a call from Officer Martel. Seems he feels slighted that a woman would put him in his place."

I opened my mouth to defend myself, but Sam's chuckle stopped me. He continued. "I don't know why. His mama and grandmama kept most of the ohana in line with a look." A soft laugh traveled across the line. "Good women. If I didn't know better, I'd think he was adopted." His voice trailed off. "For us, it means his boxers got in a knot."

"So, I've made an enemy?" I asked, guilty.

"Far from it. Martel and the rest of the boys know better than to mess with you or try anything sneaky. Don't hold it against them. If I were in their place, I'd try the same thing. If they do make another appearance, don't let their shadow fall on you. Just move along and give me a call, okay?"

"Okay," Zelda said but rolled her eyes. We were not used to men taking care of things for us. Saying they would, yes. But doing it was another matter entirely. She clicked off the phone, and we settled into the couch with a sigh.

"Why do I feel like I've been chastised?" I leaned my head against the back of the wicker sofa.

"Because you were," Zelda replied in a matter-of-fact tone. "Never forget, it doesn't matter how evolved or whatever, men are inherently scared of strong women."

I scrunched up my face. "I don't know about that, Zel."

The bag crinkled as Zelda reached for the chips. "Three words: They burned witches." She nodded knowingly. "Maybe not all men…but most men are intimidated by strong women. Outspoken women."

I nodded, not one hundred percent in agreement. My thoughts traveled to my ex-boyfriend back home, Scott. We had left on decent terms, friends, at least. He was a police detective and could give me insight. But would he? Or would he tell me to stay out of it like he did the last time I got involved in something and ended up almost dying?

I pulled his contact up on my phone and stared at his name for a long time before I realized Zelda had been talking.

"What?" I asked.

"You haven't been listening, have you?" She pursed her lips. "I could have confessed to murder, and here you are daydreaming."

I shook my head. "You would never confess to murder; you would not do well in prison."

"This is true." She shivered. "The confinement, beige, the noise." She shivered again.

"What were you saying?" I dropped my phone on the couch, picked it back up, and put it face down, hoping to resist temptation.

"That you got out of the rest of the tours after all." She smiled. "I'm sorry I booked so much. I should have taken into consideration where you were and not pushed."

I shook my head. "Don't worry about it."

"And I'm sorry I've slept with half the resort."

I flew to a seated position so fast, I almost fell off the couch. "What? How did you do that? When?"

She shrugged, rolling her shoulders in. "When you were resting. I would go for walks or whatever."

"And what? Your pants would just fall off?"

Color rose in her cheeks. "Lex, that's ridiculous. It's not like I was down in the lobby waving my business around."

My voice rose. "Weren't you?"

"Okay, maybe saying I slept with half the resort is a bit of an exaggeration. It's not like I..." She let the words fall. I had forgotten how much Zelda had been through, just as much as me, even if she didn't have the physical scars. She would carry the mental and emotional scars for a while, and they weren't so quick to heal. Would she ever be able to trust herself in a relationship again? Knowing someone you shared a bed with was a serial killer did a number on anyone. Part of me wanted to blame her free ways for getting us in this situation, but I knew it was deeper than that.

"I know you weren't strutting your stuff out on the corner, but still, you don't have to follow every urge, you know?"

She nodded meekly. "Sometimes, it's just..." She huffed. "I was here by myself and felt so alone." She crossed her arms over her chest. "I guess I'm not in the best place."

I pushed the chips aside to lean over to wrap my arms around her. "We'll get through this, Zelda." I sighed. "I thought I was in a better place, too. And I won't even talk about my temper."

She wiped a hand across her face. "You have had a short fuse lately. Is it me and my shenanigans or something else?"

I sat quietly for a moment, contemplating the questions. Zelda was always Zelda, and I loved her just as she was. "No, it's me. I'm looking for enemies when I should be seeing friends."

"Good, use that. We need as many friends as we can find right now."

I scrunched up my face. "And maybe ones we haven't slept with?"

Zelda grabbed a pillow and threw it at my head. Just as it made contact, I let out a dramatic scream. Laughter ensued from both of us.

Chapter Eleven

"Let's head down to the lounge and see if a memory sparks about the other night," I suggested and moved to stand. Zelda stayed on the sofa. One glance at her bitten lip told me she wasn't thrilled with the idea. I groaned and pulled her up. "Come on, it'll be good. Then we can go to the beach, okay?"

Her slight nod was enough of an agreement. I threw my tote bag over my shoulder, and we headed out.

The lounge was on the lower level of the main resort building, giving it a hideaway, cave-like feel. An entire wall opened to the ocean, and the dense but meticulously manicured tropical gardens reached inside. The whole place hummed with energy as the servers glided around, serving other guests and taking orders.

A server moved past us with a tray full of drinks. The tall glasses blocked his face. Zelda's brow scrunched.

"What's up? You're offended by alcohol now?" I teased.

She shook her head. "No, that server. He looks familiar, but I don't know from where."

We took seats at a high-top table in the middle of the room. A server came and took our order. Mai Tai for me and a Samuri Sling for Zelda. Since I'd made good on cutting back on the prescription meds a couple nights ago, I looked forward to a strong drink.

"Do you want to try those cheese balls Koa mentioned?" I inquired after tucking my tote bag on the empty seat.

She let out a deep sigh and rested her forearms on the table. "Yeah, and whatever other appetizers they may offer." She reached for the menu. "I have a feeling it's going to be a long afternoon."

I couldn't disagree. The lounge had to be an uncomfortable place for Zelda. "We'll get through this together," I promised her, and we ordered goat cheese balls, spring rolls, and bruschetta when the server brought our drinks.

She and I talked about nothing and everything while we sipped our drinks and enjoyed the warm Hawaiian breeze. I wanted to give her time to relax before she had to recall the events of the night of the murder.

We were laughing about something random when I felt a warm, firm hand on my back. I turned to see Koa behind us. My heart fluttered, and I couldn't prevent the smile that spread across my face.

"Koa, join us." Zelda gave him a playful smack on the shoulder and gestured to the chair next to her.

He hopped onto the chair. "I like when everyone is happy to see me."

As a cloud passed outside, an odd thought crossed my mind. Koa said he told Sam he didn't come to the lounge very often, yet he showed up here shortly after Zelda and I arrived. Interesting. My heart still raced; now I wasn't sure if it was attraction or fear.

The server delivered the food. "You mean happy to see food," Zelda joked.

"Whatever," he teased, before ordering a juice.

Zelda picked through plates of food, sniffing and

dabbing her finger in accompanying sauces before tasting them. I playfully smacked her hand. "Glad we're concerned about manners."

She stuck her tongue out at me.

I grabbed a cheese ball and popped it in my mouth. The warm, savory flavor exploded against my taste buds, sending me into a happy dance in my seat.

"It's good, right?" Koa asked. All I could do was nod around a mouthful. "This cheese is from here on the island. There's a farm up in the mountains. Someday, we'll have to head up there."

I glanced at Zelda, and her head was down as she faked attention on the food, but her gaze took Koa and I in through the mass of curls on her head. I suppressed a huge smile. The scene reminded me of one from middle school where Zelda bent over backwards, even got detention, so I could say hello to a boy I liked. Unfortunately, the boy never knew I existed, even after all the trouble she went to. Gotta say, you have a best friend, you have it all.

After the server brought another round of appetizers and water, Koa spoke. "Want to know what I found, or should we order dessert first?"

"I'd love a sweet, but right now, facts would be preferred." I took a bite of a spring roll and crunched down on the veggies and seafood filling.

"Okay, I'll get you something sweet later." Koa winked in my direction, and fire rose across my chest and up to my hairline.

Zelda choked a cough down. "Wow, that drink is catching up with me." She twisted her head side to side. "I'll be back." She was on the way to the bathroom before I could protest.

I cleared my throat. "Why do you show up at the oddest times?" I heard the tremor in my voice. "Like you know where we are?"

"We should wait until Zelda gets back." Koa's voice fell an octave.

"No, we're not waiting, and you're not deflecting." My knuckles whitened as I gripped the arms of the wicker chair. A small smile played on the corners of his lips. I tried not to stare at the thick mustache above it.

His fingers bounced on the table. "I came down here to follow a lead."

My eyebrow rose. "A lead you didn't mention?"

He sighed. "I've always worked alone. It didn't occur to me to tell you until it panned out."

That was plausible and too convenient. I wasn't sold but nodded like I understood.

"Let's be honest? It would be easier if you both stayed out of it." Fire erupted in my belly and my fists clenched.

Koa continued. "But I understand that won't happen. I'll give you a better heads-up next time."

I exhaled hard and smiled. Did he agree too easily, or am I paranoid? I reminded myself I had to trust Koa for Zelda's sake. "Fine." I crossed my arms and threw a glance towards the bathrooms. "Another thing, no more lunch, dinner dates, or anything else—until Zelda is in the clear. Got it? She's all I have time for."

"So, no time to ravage you?"

"What?"

The words came out as a scream before I realized it. My hands flew to my mouth as Koa threw his head back and laughed. It was one of the best sounds I had ever heard. I dissolved into giggles, out of embarrassment, but really laughed after a few moments.

Zelda returned to the table wearing a confused look on her face. "What did I miss?"

That made us laugh harder. We were bent over, holding our stomachs. No sound came out of our mouths, just gasping for air. Zelda stared at us, wide-eyed, and took her seat, awkward and out of place. "Let me know when you're done," she said with a laugh and reached for a cheeseball.

Breathless, I settled against the chair, overwhelmed with emotions. I must get a handle on them.

"Can we talk about me now?"

We nodded, suppressing another giggling fit. "Whenever you're ready."

Zelda crossed her arms over herself and pursed her lips, containing her own laughter.

We stopped laughing, would catch our breath, and start again. After several minutes, our laughter slowed. And being the middle-aged woman I am, I excused myself to the bathroom before we could go further.

I settled against the back of the chair and silence fell around the table. To one side, a man in a Hawaiian shirt sat up to play music. More people filtered in, and the click of glasses accented the waves just outside. Koa smacked his thighs with his hands and sighed. "Well, let me start."

"Whenever." Zelda spun the orange and cherry on the drink garnish.

"The witness." His words fell heavy on us. "His name is Shane Lincoln and says he knows what happened at the beach and that he saw you that evening in the lounge when Jeff was murdered."

"How is that possible?" I asked and thought back to

the day everything began. "It has to be someone on the tour and staying here, doesn't it?"

Koa shrugged. "I've checked everyone on the tour. All were tourists. Most have already left the islands. He's a local. Mid-twenties."

My hand found the bottom seam on my top, and I began to absently trace it with my fingers.

Zelda tapped her finger on the table. "I don't remember recognizing anyone that night."

"Not that you could have with whatever drugs were in your system," I reminded her.

Koa nodded. "That concerns me. Seems too convenient."

It was handy. Too much so. Koa seemed to be everywhere and had an answer for everything. I threw a loaded glance at him. "Lots of things are too convenient."

Koa opened his mouth, but Zelda interrupted. "Did Sam tell you the sheriff stopped by today? To chat?"

He snorted. "No law enforcement person ever shows up just to talk, Zelda. That's like saying you go to a fast-food restaurant for the vegetables."

I couldn't think of the last time I ate a vegetable besides fries at a drive thru. "Why do you think the sheriff showed up?"

Koa leaned back with a sigh. "That's a good question. He shouldn't have."

My fingers traced the condensation on my glass as I attempted to get my thoughts in order. "Seems risky, or downright stupid. So, I'm no expert like you are, but why would the head of the local sheriff department come by…what…to make an appearance?" I shrugged. "He wasn't here to say howdy."

Zelda rolled her eyes. "That's for damn sure."

I continued, "Then why do it? He accomplished nothing and served no purpose."

"That is the outcome of most men." Zelda threw back the last of her drink.

Koa shrugged. "Maybe he wanted to show you their presence. Or he thought he would catch you off guard and get a lead. The artifact still hasn't been found."

Despite the warm breeze, an icy chill swept through me. "Could someone have killed Jeff for the artifact? Is it valuable?"

He pinched the bridge of his nose. "Invaluable. Not only to Hawaiian culture, but monetarily as well. The material it's made from is rare."

Zelda sat forward, forearms on table. "Wait, I thought it was made of lava rock?"

"That's a common misbelief. It's made from an unknown material." It was my turn for my eyebrows to raise. Koa continued. "Might be because no testing has been allowed on it in decades. Or it was a gift from the gods. Some cable television show even tried to say it was from an alien civilization."

"And it's not been found…" Zelda's eyes widened.

My nerves jumped as Zelda and my eyes met. "That means something, right?"

Koa glanced down at his lap, not meeting my gaze. "It could. Could be if she had an airtight alibi and the police stopped right there. These people do good work. But we still have a body to account for."

My jaw clenched. "One thing at a time."

"Is any alibi airtight?" Zelda asked, leaned forward again.

Koa shook his head. "Nothing is airtight. Even

though no weapon has been found, no one will forget the body was found in your bed. DNA might show another person in the room, but in this case that doesn't matter."

She nodded. "My DNA isn't on him." She glanced at me. "Probably."

"There was too much DNA evidence recovered from the scene," he said. "It happens in a hotel room, no matter how clean. It'll take weeks, maybe months, to get the results back, and even longer to sort it all out."

"Another question I didn't want to ask…" Zelda cleared her throat. "What killed him?'

I stared at her in surprise. The stab wounds caused death, but it never occurred to me to ask about the weapon. Where was my mind?

"He was stabbed several times with a yet unidentified object. It entered the mid torso between the first and second ribs. Punctured the heart and lungs. He bled out. When you found him, Lexi, he was already long dead."

"Why didn't he scream or cry out?" I asked.

He shrugged, but Zelda answered. "Maybe someone slipped him something?"

Something nagged at the base of my skull. "How does someone get stabbed to death in our condo, and no one hears anything? Zelda didn't because of the drugs she was slipped, but I can't get over that someone saw or heard something. It doesn't feel right." I wasn't going to voice it aloud, but I still didn't understand why I hadn't heard anything.

"I agree. There's only one answer to all our questions right now."

Zelda and I sat on the edge of our seats, waiting.

"And?" I couldn't take it another moment.

"There's another player involved, and they've got some resources."

Zelda's curls bounced in agreement. "Right! And they're framing me for murder."

Chapter Twelve

Koa let out a dry laugh. "Who do you think is trying to frame you?"

Zelda shrugged. "Beats me. All I know is there was a dead man in my bed, and I had nothing to do with it. You don't have to be a rocket scientist to figure out someone else is involved."

"Right, but who?" Koa asked. "Who has the motive to frame you? Other than Lexi and her folks, does anyone know you're on the island?"

"You would have to be an idiot to think someone else wasn't involved," I scoffed.

Zelda shook her head. "I've met a few people recently." Her voice lowered. "But no one I've ticked off or anything."

I looked away, not wanting to betray my emotions. It wasn't right for me to judge her. We had given that up a couple decades ago, but I couldn't shake the thought her behavior got her into this situation.

"Would anyone back home have reasons to frame you?"

We both shook our heads. "No enemies above ground," Zelda said.

I had to give Koa credit for not flinching. "Then that frame train isn't leaving the station."

"Wait." I almost jumped out of the chair. "The artifact is worth money, right? What if there wasn't a motive? What if Jeff dying in Zelda's bed was the symptom of something that went bad?"

Mouth grim, Koa stared at me for several seconds before letting out a low whistle. "You may be onto something there."

"You think Jeff ending up in my bed was all by chance?" Zelda asked.

"Maybe…" My hands spread out in a helpless gesture. I wanted to say more, but it would give too much information to Koa.

Zelda let out a breathy sigh. "So let me get this straight. I'm being framed by an incompetent murderer? Great."

"Things could have gone wrong, and you were the easy way out."

"I am easy," Zelda joked and finished the last spring roll.

Koa ignored our joke and tapped his fingers on the edge of the table. "I don't like it, but I agree. I did a background check, and Jeff came up too clean. Everything he told Zelda was true."

"Oh, like a fake identity?" Zelda asked.

"Not exactly, more like nothing in his life has been interesting or exceptional. Sure, some people are just average, but most have something interesting in their lives. Some little 'ah ha!' fact that explains things." He shook his head. "He had nothing. Only child, average grades, majored in business in college, went to work for his mom's company. She died when he was in his thirties, leaving the business to him. He cashed it out a couple months ago."

"Would you say mundane to the point of hiding something perhaps?"

Koa raised an eyebrow. "Perhaps." He pointed a finger at Zelda. "Stay as far away from people as possible, unless they're providing some sort of service." He stopped. "Paid and legal services both," he clarified.

I chuckled. He had caught on to Zelda.

She perked up. "We should check out the museum again."

Koa winced. "How about I take that one? Not sure you should go back there, Zelda."

Her face reddened. "It's not the first museum I've been banned from."

We dissolved in laughter as she regaled us with a story of the time she got herself banned from the local Pioneer Trails Museum after strenuously questioning the language used in a display.

Koa asked a couple more questions that sounded rather mundane. After a few minutes, we called it a day, charged everything to the room, and left a generous tip.

The scent of plumeria mingled with the salty air as we wandered along the manicured pathways of the resort back to our condo. Swaying palm trees cast dappled shadows on the vibrant hibiscus flowers that lined the path. A contented sigh escaped me. This was the type of evening I could get used to for the rest of my life.

As soon as we entered the room, Zelda stretched. Big and fake. "Ugh, I'm so tired, going to bed. Good night." She threw me a glance at her door, made a kissy face, and pointed at the back of Koa's head. I rolled my eyes.

He turned to Zelda, and she darted into her room, slamming the door. He turned back to me with a smile. "She's a character, isn't she?"

"Wouldn't be her if she wasn't." I shrugged, long

ago accepting her and her ways.

"Something to get used to," Koa said, his gaze on the floor, his fingers bouncing on his leg.

"Not everyone can." I willed him to meet my eyes. "It takes effort."

"But worth it." He stared out the doors at the garden grounds and the ocean beyond. Silence grew between us. "Worth it to get to know you better."

I bit my tongue and suppressed a smile. Now my eyes avoided his. I was sure he could see my heart beating out of my chest. I cleared my throat and searched for words.

"Well, I better head out." Koa slapped his legs and moved to the door. I scrambled out of the way, and we found ourselves close together, a pleasant warmth radiating between us. My breath came in hitches. Our eyes met, and the world stopped. Our lips touched, and an electric shock flowed through me, unlike anything I could have ever imagined.

I tumbled into him, and our arms wrapped around each other, clutching at fabric, and threatening to burst at seams. I was pulled into the deepest ocean and didn't care. Suddenly, my heart raced out of my chest. I pushed Koa away and gulped for air.

We stepped away from each other. He exhaled hard, his breath washed over me, and I had to fight the urge to throw my arms around him again and give myself to him, totally and completely.

Koa nodded, cleared his throat, and opened the door. "Lock this door behind me," he said, his voice husky.

Rooted to the spot, I could only manage a jerky nod as he vanished from sight. The scent of Koa lingered in the air—a clean soapiness entwined with a deeper, richer musk. It mingled with the heady perfume of plumeria and the salty tang of the ocean, a bittersweet reminder of his presence even as the world seemed to tilt on its axis.

Never in my forty-plus years had I experienced anything like that. Not with my first short-lived marriage, or any of the relationships before and since. I stumbled to the bedroom in a daze and changed into a light cotton pioneer nightgown covering me from head to toe.

I wasn't a fan of romance novels; they never seem realistic. Those life-changing relationships, connections that would burn so hot they could change the course of lives and the world. None of it was real. People didn't have those experiences outside of books and movies. I lay in bed and watched the shadows dance on the ceiling, unable to sleep. Could it be these feelings exist, or was it all this otherworldly place and emotions influencing the situation? I had been through so much. After everything, it wasn't possible to have found love.

Yet, the electricity still flowed across my lips. I turned on my side and punched the pillow. He made a life here in Hawaii. I had resolved that my life, and Zelda's, would be growing old together with a few pets back in Atherton. As I drifted off to sleep, I wondered if there just might be more to life than growing old with my best friend.

Chapter Thirteen

I drifted awake, greeted by a gentle caress of a golden sun. The light blankets and sheets tangled around my legs. The memory of the kiss with Koa last night still sent tingles through me. Not just deep in my body, but there in a tiny flutter of my heart. I cursed. This was not the time for teenage crushes and throbbing body parts.

I threw my legs over the edge of the bed, stomping to the bathroom. The smell of coffee and something else wafted into the room. Zelda was up and doing something in the kitchen. The flutter in my heart might be more of a worry of whether she might burn the place down.

She stood in the kitchenette in an oversized T-shirt featuring a pineapple character with the words "Happy Pineapple Day." Her hair was a chaotic mass of curls that stood up in all directions. She glanced up as I walked in. "Good morning, Sunshine, thought I'd make coffee." She pointed to the small pot on the back of the counter. "One hundred percent Kona coffee." She gave me a side eye as I reached for a cup and poured the coffee.

"Are you cooking something? I haven't seen any smoke yet, so I wasn't sure," I joked.

"Ha ha. I can do something in the kitchen," Zelda replied. "I got up early and went down to the restaurant. Picked up some pastries and bacon. Just warming it up in this little toaster oven. I bought more than enough for the two of us." She bent to look around me into the open door of my bedroom. "Will we have extra, or do we have a guest?"

I frowned. "No guests. I don't think the sheriff has started stationing an officer in our rental to watch over you. Yet."

A sly smile played at the corner of her lips as she opened the little door of the air fryer and pulled the pastries out. "Give it time, give it time. I was hoping a certain tall, dark, and handsome man would be…shall we say, investigating privately last night."

I added sugar and a heavy hand of creamer to the coffee before taking a seat at the small dining table. "Uh-huh." And took a sip of coffee. With hints of chocolate, it was smooth.

Zelda remained quiet, a feat for her, but I sensed her desire to ask a million and one questions. She brought a plate loaded with pastries and crispy bacon to the table, with an enormous coffee cup.

"This is enough for a large family." I took a round, sugar covered pastry, tore it open. Bright orange filling spilled out.

"I think that's mango," Zelda commented, as she tore into one and white cream spilled out. She took a bite, chewed and moaned.

I took a bite of mine and had to agree it was delightful. "What flavor is yours?"

Zelda shook her head. "No idea, but it's yum. I don't know the last time I had a pastry." She finished in a few bites. As good as it was, I picked at mine, using sips of coffee to cover my lack of appetite. Zelda had started on her third before she noticed. "What's going on? Mr. Mustache not packing a semi?" she asked in all seriousness.

The blank look on my face encouraged her to continue. "Like a semi-automatic gun? You know, like, is that a gun in your pocket, or are you happy to see me?" she said in a faux accent of undetermined origin.

I rolled my eyes. "We just kissed, that's all," I said, my tone guarded. "And you know all those donuts are going to wreck your stomach."

She shrugged. "Oh, I know it. And it'll be worth every bit." Zelda's stare searched over me, for what I didn't know. We didn't keep many secrets, but the way the kiss made me feel, I wasn't sure I wanted to talk about it. At least not yet. Kisses like that didn't happen to women like me. Zelda shrugged and finished her coffee, wiping a napkin across her mouth. "Whatever happened, if it woke you up, I'm happy for it."

I frowned. "What?"

Zelda turned to me. "I know what you went through was a lot, and I don't want to demean it, but at some point, you have to take a step forward. Stop sleepwalking through life."

I sat the coffee cup down and crossed my arms over my chest. "You mean move on like nothing happened? So everyone else is happy?"

She sighed hard and as she leaned back in the chair, the wicker creaked. "That's not what I mean at all. I'll be brutal here, Lex. You are always going to carry what happened with you. Always. We all carry our past with us. It doesn't fall away like a lizard shedding its skin. But we also carry our past joys and successes, and you've had more than a few of those. I want you to remember those, too. All that makes up who you are too."

As she spoke, tears came to my eyes. Had I only been half living these past few months? I knew she was right.

"But at some point, take a step to the future or—" she stopped and stared out to the ocean beyond, her face set grimly, "—stagnate. Stagnation is death. Those are your choices." She let her words fall in the room, and silence filled the space between us. After a while, she got up without another word and went into her room.

I stayed at the table for a long time, till the coffee went cold. Zelda rarely chastised me, but when she did, it was a swift kick in the butt. She was right, of course. I'd been living in a fog. I blamed it on the medications and lingering pain, but it was more than that. I was afraid of moving forward and living again. I put my coffee cup in the kitchen, heard the shower turn on in Zelda's bathroom, and figured I should do the same.

An hour later, and enough positive self-talk to fill a book, I emerged from my bedroom to find Zelda in a swimsuit and coverup. "I see you're comfortable with the ankle bracelet?" I inquired.

She struck a pin-up pose on the couch, hand behind the head, lips pursed. "What? This doesn't go with my suit?" She laughed and shook her head. "Not sure I could hide it if I wanted too. Ready to hit the beach?" She reached for her bag.

I nodded and grabbed a few things off the table, my sunglasses and such, and stuffed them in my bag. "I read you can wrap tin foil around them and mess with the signal, but the last thing I need is the sheriff further up my behind." She grabbed a couple water bottles from the small fridge, and we headed out.

As soon as our feet hit the sand, resort employees ran over each other to pull loungers up for us, angle the umbrellas just right, lay our towels out, and ensure we had sunblock and water. Once we were settled, I turned to Zelda. "Why are they so attentive? I don't see anyone else get half the attention we do."

She smiled and turned towards me. "They think I'm a cougar on the prowl and capable of murder." She wagged her eyebrows behind her sunglasses. "Does wonders for their hustle when they think they might be next. Whether in my bed or their grave is unclear."

"Zelda!"

She laughed. "Calm down, Lex. I tip well and often. They've gotten to know it, and it's worth the money. The extra service makes me feel special."

I gave her a prune face and leaned back in the lounger. Another group of tourists sat near us, coolers overflowing with ice, speaker playing country music quietly to the side. Beer cans stacked in the sand. All before noon.

She was right. I had to stop sleepwalking.

But could I ever be free?

Chapter Fourteen

I stared at a group of tourists playing cornhole in the sand. Laughter drifted on the breeze for a long time before I willed myself to reply.

She made a sound of mixed frustration and disgust. "The man *likes* you. Text him before I turn fifty. Jeeze."

I rolled my eyes behind the sunglasses. "Let's go explore the beach and those woods. I want to see what it was that might have attacked Jeff."

Zelda nodded. "Let's take another dip and go change."

We pulled ourselves up and sauntered into the ocean, where the waves hit our legs and cooled our sun-warmed skin. We floated and swam out far enough to see the mountains in the distance behind the resort. After a while, we made our way back to the beach chairs and the condo.

It didn't take us long to change and head out in the car. The Black Sand Beach was on the southern tip of the island and easy to find. We parked in a large lot and got out. Signs lead to the beach, lava tunnel, hiking trails, and a restaurant. My stomach grumbled. We headed in the direction of the restaurant first.

Fish tacos and pineapple slaw satisfied us and gave us energy to explore. The beach featured sun worshipers and surfers. We walked past them to the trail that led to the lava tube.

"After you." I held out a hand for her to take the lead.

She smiled. "Beauty before age?"

I shoved her playfully on the shoulder. "Get in there."

The verdant jungle woods engulfed us. I understood how initially Zelda couldn't make out who Jeff spoke to. The path forked, and the sign pointed to the right for the lava tube. Zelda stopped.

"Do you remember which way you went?"

She nodded. "Yeah, this way. Towards the left." I followed.

The path appeared more overgrown and less traveled. We swatted bugs away and smacked them on our arms and legs. The sooner I could be out of here, the better. It wasn't much longer until the path opened, revealing a small lava tube. I huffed. "This wasn't on the tour."

"No." Zelda was behind me as we walked into the heavier woods. "I was heading in this direction when I heard the voices."

I glanced around the small clearing. We barely fit, as the thick foliage reached out to us. It would be hard for more than two people to be here. "Stop right where you were that day, Zel. Does my voice sound like Jeff's?"

"No, too close."

I back up closer to the black hole of the lava tube. "Now?"

"Eh, almost?"

I turned the flashlight on my phone on and shined it into the tube. Nothing but black rock. I stepped inside. "How about now?"

"That's it," Zelda said excitedly and entered the clearing. "Why would he be in the lava tube? I mean, it's cool and all, but…why?"

I didn't answer but searched the inside with the flashlight. My battery was okay, but my signal was dead. I stepped outside the tube and the signal returned. "No signal in there. Maybe that has something to do with it?"

The flashlight was still on when Zelda screamed. She ran to a rock outcropping near the mouth of the tube. The flashlight glinted off something shiny. Zelda bent over and reached for the shiny object imbedded in the lush greenery.

With my heart racing in my chest, I knew what it was before she unwrapped it. Her gaze wide and mouth agape as she opened her palm to show the artifact in her hand.

It was a rough-looking triangular object, about six inches in length. Its base was broad and flat, while the opposite end tapered to a sharp, almost crystalline point. Zelda turned it over in her hand. The smooth, translucent surface glowed with an iridescent sheen as the colors shifted in the light. Koa was right. It certainly wasn't made from lava rock.

"Crap," I said breathlessly. So much talk about this thing, and now to have it in front of me, I was speechless. This was the thing that was supposed to give eternal life and people had killed for.

Zelda held it out to me. "Yeah, crap. I don't want to hold it." She waved it towards me. "What do I do?"

"Then why the hell did you pick it up?" I chastised her, not sure what we should do with it. We couldn't leave it here.

She waved the thing at me again. "Excitement? I

don't know. Do something."

I stared around the clearing and grabbed a handful of green plants. "Let's wrap it up in this and put it in my bag." I stuffed it into my tote. Out of sight and safe for the moment.

Zelda let out a sigh of relief. "Okay, let's get out of here."

The entire walk back, my throat constricted, and my breath strained. In the car, we turned the air conditioning to high and sat in the cool breeze for a while.

Zelda stared straight ahead. "Do we turn this into the police?"

"Uh." I leaned my head back. "No. And we don't tell Koa and Sam either."

Zelda's sharp intake of breath relayed her anxiety. The silence grew until she nodded. "Trust no one."

My face grim, I nodded and put the car in gear. "We need a stiff drink and the ocean."

"That's for damn sure."

We returned to the resort and were met by the head of security at the resort gate. Keawe's dark gaze narrowed when he saw us. "Ladies. Out on an excursion?"

Our smiles were tense and small. "Just sightseeing." I took my foot off the brake and the car rolled forward.

"Whoa now." He held a hand in front of the windshield. Zelda cursed under her breath. "How were the fish tacos?" He rested an arm on the car door, holding us hostage.

"Delightful. As was the coleslaw. But you know, all that cheese is going right through me, and I'd hate to pay an additional cleaning fee for the rental car, so if you'd excuse us." I wasn't sure if it was shock or the fear of what might happen, but Keawe dropped his arm as we rolled away.

"Whew, for a minute there I thought I was going to mess up this seat. That man is creepy, and I know creepy." Zelda glanced in the side mirror as we parked. "Is he tracking the ankle bracelet?"

I parked and we wandered through the hotel to our condo. "Possibly, but how did he know what we ordered?"

Zelda shrugged. "It is one of the most popular things on the menu, maybe a good guess?"

"Seems a little too convenient for my taste."

After a quick stop to the bathroom, we headed to the beach. Before leaving the condo, I debated about where to hide the artifact in the safest place I could think of, the drawer with my socks, underwear, and bras. Instead, I threw the leaves away, wrapped it in an old shirt, and stuffed it in the bottom of my tote. It would never leave my side.

Zelda and I spent the rest of the day on the resort beach. The staff made sure to keep us hydrated and full while we read, napped, and played in the surf. I never looked once at the clock, or my phone, and pushed the thoughts of the artifact aside. The time filled my soul and gave us energy.

We headed back to the room, and I changed into shorts and a round-necked collared T-shirt before Koa texted to say he was free and on his way to the condo. I dropped on the couch. Part of me was thrilled to see Koa. Another part knew we couldn't trust anyone, even Mr. Stache. My thoughts were broken when the bedroom door flew open.

Zelda stood there in an oversized kitten T-shirt and

shorts, hair astray from sleep, eyes wide. "We have a problem."

A knock at the door interrupted her explanation. I held up my hand to silence her.

"I feel like that's not the first time you've said that." Koa had come up to the room.

Zelda ignored him and waved her cell phone in my face. I grabbed the phone from her hand. "What?"

I stared at the screen, which showed a tabloid website featuring a story about an ultra-rich, reclusive tech genius named Ashley Cregg. I handed the phone back towards her. "What does this have to do with us?"

She rolled her eyes. "Read the article. It says this Ashley Cregg is a billionaire who has a son named Jeff Parks who happened to be found dead in an unnamed woman's bed."

My blood froze. "Oh shit, Zel. You're the unnamed woman."

"Be careful talking about Cregg," he said, and grabbed her phone. He shuffled between apps and screens before he handed it back.

She grabbed the phone back and stared at the screen. "Hey, where's the article?"

He frowned. "Not only do you need to be careful about who hears you talking about Cregg," Koa said, "but also doing an internet search for him using hotel Wi-Fi. Guaranteed red flag."

I frowned. "Why would that matter?"

He owns the hotel."

My jaw dropped and I froze in disbelief. "He owns the hotel? *And* he's Jeff's dad?"

Koa had pulled out his phone and flipped between applications. "And half the island. Hold on, let me pull up a VPN. It's not traceable. Or at least harder than the hotel system is."

Zelda groaned and dropped onto the couch. "I'm going to prison. There's no way I'm going to get out of this."

"Zelda, nothing has changed," I said. "You still didn't commit murder."

"You're right about that, but now I'm up against a billionaire."

Koa leaned against the wall and stared intently at his phone. The silence crackled with nervous energy, like storm brewing below the surface. I found a string at the hem of my shorts and twisted it between my fingers.

Koa finished reading, dropping the phone to his side. "I don't like being blindsided." His jaw worked. "The father of the man Zelda found in her bed, dead, just so happens to be the same man that owns most of the island."

Zelda scoffed. "When you say it aloud, it sounds really bad. Like horrible."

My positivity tanked, and I agreed with Zelda. None of this sounded good, but there was something there. "Hold on, what if the dad had something to do with it?" Their questioning gazes turned on me. "Something went bad between them," I shrugged. "Family, you know? Jeff ends up dead, and the dad couldn't imagine just discarding the body, throwing it into the ocean or whatever."

Koa stroked his chin. "Or he hired someone to do it, and it went south, and they tried to cover it up."

I stood, ready to grab my tote and find the man. "We must talk to Cregg somehow. And soon."

Koa held out his hands in frustration and sighed.

"That's easier said than done."

I rested a fist on my cocked hip. "What? You're a detective, find him."

"Everyone knows where he lives. It's a matter of getting in. You don't just walk into Ashley Cregg's compound."

"We'll see about that." I rolled my eyes. "I don't have much to lose right now, and I'm going to find him and talk to him."

Koa threw his hands up. "Fine. But at least wait until the morning, after breakfast. Going over there now, worked up, won't help."

The room thrummed with unspoken tension. I inhaled and nodded.

Zelda cleared her throat. "So, this Cregg fella is pretty powerful, huh?

He shook his head. "No one likes the man. He swooped in a few years ago with all his money, bought up the locals' land, and pushed them out. Their homeland." His voice raised and his face colored. "If anything, it works against him. What worries me is he has so much money…"

My cheeks blew out with frustration. "None of this is inspiring confidence."

Koa kept pacing. "Finding out the truth is much harder, and that's our first priority."

"We've got to find the connection between Jeff and whoever killed him," I said. "Like Koa said, we must find the truth and clear your name. That's priority one."

"In the morning, first thing." Koa stopped and stared at Zelda and I on the couch.

My blood warmed.

"Does that mean you'll be spending the night?"

Zelda asked, too chipper.

My mouth dropped open, and I turned to stare at her. "Zelda!"

"What?" She shrugged. "Simple question."

I glanced at Koa; his face was as flushed as I imagined mine was now, too. He fidgeted with his leather belt and cleared his throat. "I should be going. I'll see you in the morning." At the door he nodded to both of us before he closed it behind himself.

"Zelda!" I reached across the small couch and smacked her arm, not altogether playfully. "How dare you?"

"What?" She pulled away from me and laughed. The smile was slow to leave her face. "It's good to see you smile. And blush." She stared at me for a long time. "You like him?"

I shrugged. "I'm not sure. Attracted, definitely."

"Then go with it, see where it goes. I don't want to hear a peep about how this isn't the time or you're too busy saving me *again* or other foolishness." She winked and pulled me to standing. "Come on, let's get a good night's sleep so you are fresh and ready for your man."

Chapter Fifteen

I was up before the sun and closed the door of the condo quietly so not to disturb Zelda. The resort was tranquil. The swimming pools, which would teem with activity as the day progressed, were now still and reflective, mirroring the starlit sky. Empty lounge chairs stood on the pristine white sand beach, their cushions damp with the night dew.

The rental car was parked in the self-park lot, a short walk from the main entrance. I got in and pulled up directions for the *Wai Ola* Coffee Farm on the navigation system.

Disregarding, Koa's warning, I had discovered an online chat between locals about how Ashley Cregg used the farm as a front for his compound. I could drive to the farm and take their tour, just like anyone else. Since the first tour started at seven, I had enough time to grab a coffee and breakfast sandwich at the roadside stand on the way.

A short time later, as the first rays of sunlight reached me, I was heading south on the main highway. The nav system said the farm was on the south side of the island. Interesting. Not far from where the lava tube and beach were where Zelda and I found the artifact. I wondered if there was a connection.

Following the GPS, I directed the car off the blacktop onto a well-maintained gravel road a few minutes later. A small, long wooden building came into view. The green paint blended into the verdant landscape surrounding it. I slowed and parked next to the small SUVs and sports cars. The sun was barely up, and the coolness of the night had dissipated. It left me sticky and warm, and I pulled the oversized T-shirt away from my chest.

Other tourists milled about the front of the building as employees brought out cases of fresh fruit and avocados. I studied them seriously until they brought out locally made banana bread, and then all thoughts went out the window. I paid for two loaves, still warm from the oven, and shoved them into my tote. It was becoming heavier every day.

"If you're here for the tour, let's get going." A tall, lanky man in a green T-shirt featured the farm's name "*Wai Ola*" in decorative script. The tourists in their khaki shorts or athletic leggings huddled around as the man began a descriptive and deep history of the coffee bean on the island.

The group moved through ankle tall grass as the tour through the farm continued. We inspected the milling facilities and oohed and aahed at the dehulling, roasting, and grinding of the beans. Roasting wasn't scheduled for the day, but we nodded as the man explained the small batch process. My curiosity gave way to a touch of apprehension as we entered the coffee grove. Was I close to Cregg's compound? Would I be able to get to it?

Sun filtered through emerald-colored leaves, dappling a path through rows of coffee trees. Ripe red cherries hung heavy on their branches; the sweet, earthy aroma filled the air. The breeze rustled leaves and birds chirped, a symphony amidst the green giants.

A middle-aged man squatted and picked something off the ground. With a grunt, he stood and examined his find. "Hey, hey! Can we eat these?"

The tour guide didn't miss a beat. "Absolutely. Those avocados are as fresh as they get." He turned back to the group, who all now stared at the ground. "Folks. Folks? Let's head down this row." He waved an arm to direct the group. We followed, delayed by a few people who stooped over, stuffing avocados in their pockets. At the end of the row, the tour guide turned to us and started a speech on sustainable farming. I was giving up all hope of the Cregg compound being close when another tourist interrupted the guide.

"Is that a bathroom?" she inquired, a hand over her forehead to block the nonexistent rays of sun. Through the trees in the distance was a large white structure. A big house or a small resort. Probably a short-term rental, I figured, and turned back to the guide. After all the coffee and pastries I'd indulged in, I wouldn't mind a bathroom myself right now.

He stepped in front of the woman as she began to head off in that direction. "No, ma'am. That is a private residence and not on the tour. We'll be back at the gift shop in a few moments."

My ears perked up. It had to be Ashley Cregg's house. I listened to the guide finish the sustainability talk and the group moved down another row, towards the gift shop. I hung back, counted to ten, turned, and ducked into the thick greenery.

It wasn't long until the vegetation opened to a manicured lawn. As I wiped my hands over my hair and clothes, bits of plant matter fell to the ground. Here, the lawn was so perfect it appeared fake. This Cregg guy really had a thing for control. "Geeze, they trim this grass with scissors."

A long, brick patio stretched the length of the house and looked over the green lawn and out to the ocean beyond. I stood quietly to take in the surroundings. The front door was to my right, and I figured the best thing to do was knock on it and introduce myself. I was about to put one foot down when a hand clamped down on my mouth.

I tried to scream and struggled for all I was worth against a steel arm that snaked around my waist. I kicked my feet, and my lips pulled back to expose my teeth and maybe take a bite. The scent of soap and something fruit choked down my airway. Panic rose in me at the thought of dying here on this perfect lawn with the scent of tropical fruits in my nose.

"Stop struggling," a steel voice said in my ear. The cold, professional tone scared me more than if they'd cursed or screamed. I twisted and turned, determined to get away.

"Mike, let the woman go." A soft, genteel voice came from the patio.

I glanced over the hand still clamped to my mouth to see a tall, willowy man dressed in all-light khaki. His hands were in his pockets, and the only thing that betrayed this was an odd scene was a disapproving frown on his face.

"Mike, really now," he chastised.

The hands left me, and air filled my lungs again. I huffed, adjusted my T-shirt, and turned to throw a death stare at Mike. The man was dressed in dark green camo, and, as quickly as he appeared, he slid back into the greenery. I blinked hard and took a step toward the spot where he'd just stood.

"Excuse me, madam?"

I turned back to the man in khakis on the patio. A smile played at the corner of his lips. "Would you care to join me for breakfast?"

My stomach rumbled, and I resisted the urge to rest a hand on it. I strode across the perfect grass. "Only if I can use your restroom first."

Chapter Sixteen

A smile broke out across his face. "I have six bathrooms; take your pick." I followed him across the patio into the house. The hallway walls were a deep teak wood, only broken by enormous pieces of modern art done in striking, eye-popping colors. The floors were covered with slate, embedded with light-colored stones and pristine white throw carpets. It was eerily like the resort, except that a sense of excessive expense hung in the air.

The man stopped at a door and opened it. "I'll meet you on the lanai, Ms. Burns." He turned and walked away, leaving me standing in front of what my mother would term a guest bathroom.

Mouth agape at the opulence of the interior, I did my business fast while marveling at the carved hand soap that smelled amazing, when I met my gaze in the mirror. "Wait a damn minute, how did he know my name?" I dried my hands slowly and ran a hand over my hair before I took a deep breath and headed out to meet him.

The tingle of laughter from the lanai caused me to slow my steps. A servant stood by the side of the table laughing with whom I had to assume was Ashley Cregg. The interaction appeared genuine, and the man in khakis seemed pleasant enough. I shook the thought away. Even a serial killer could be pleasant at times. I needed to be on my guard. Squaring my shoulders, I stepped onto the lanai.

"Hell, Mr. Ashley didn't tell me what you wanted for breakfast," the woman said to me. "Eggs and sausage, okay?" I nodded and she beamed. "Good, good. Coffee and pastries are on the table. I'll be out with your breakfasts soon."

When Ashley Cregg stood, then gave me a small bow, I resisted the urge to curtsy. The man's bearing reminded me of the older doctors I worked with early in my career. Kind, caring, with a steel underneath that could cut you at the knees.

"Welcome. Have a seat." He gestured towards the overstuffed lounge chair next to him.

"Thank you." I took the seat and focused on why I was here. "Mr. Cregg, it's nice to meet you."

He sat and his gaze met mine with a sparkle. "My apologies for Mike. He's new and sometimes gets a little…enthusiastic." Cregg's mouth twitched on the last word, and I resisted the urge to shiver.

I plastered on a smile. "No problem, Mr. Cregg."

He reached for the silver coffee pot and poured himself a cup. "How do you take your coffee?"

"Cream and sugar until it's khaki."

My fingertips found the thick weave in the chair cushion, and I traced the pattern. I didn't want to be rude, but I wasn't interested in small talk. He poured the coffee and delicately added the sugar and creamer.

I took a sip. "Perfect." I saluted him with the cup before I returned it to the table. "Mr. Cregg, I appreciate your kindness and friendliness. I'm not here for a social call."

He returned his cup to the table. "I'm aware of that, Ms. Burns. Social callers generally come through the front door."

This was why I traversed through the coffee farm and woods, but I didn't want Cregg to know how little I really knew. "You know why I'm here." It wasn't a question.

The servant brought steaming plates filled with scrambled eggs, Portuguese sausage, and fresh fruit. It all appeared mouthwatering, but there was no way my stomach would allow me to eat. Cregg thanked the woman and started to eat. I sat back in the chair and waited.

After what seemed like hours, he put the fork down and wiped a fabric napkin across his mouth. He cleared his throat before speaking. "Jeff's mother didn't like me much once the lawyers presented her with a prenup agreement." A sad smile crossed his face. "I set up a trust for him, made sure he had everything he needed." He waved a hand. "And her as well, within reason."

"Your relationship was transactional?"

He sipped his coffee before answering. "Not until Jeff was in his teens. I'm not an outwardly loving person. Jeff wanted more than I could show, but he was always taken care of."

Again, I traced the weaved ridge of the chair fabric. My family might annoy a few years off my life, but they were always there to love me. I wondered what Jeff's childhood must have been like and how it shaped him. "But you stopped taking care of him recently?"

Cregg shook his head. "The payments stopped, yes. He knew the trust would stop paying when he reached the age of forty-five. The theory being that by then he would have ample opportunity to make something of himself and have something of his own."

"Do you know why he was in Hawaii now? Did you meet with him?"

"Recently, he'd reached out more often. He'd mentioned he'd be on the island and wanted to meet up, but nothing was on my schedule. My schedule was full, but my assistant knew to move things for certain people. We never heard from him to finalize anything."

I stared out over the lawn to the beach where the waves crashed against the black boulder sized lava rocks. "Did he call you the day he passed?"

Cregg shook his head. "He texted, but I didn't respond. I was out of touch most of the day."

My ears perked up. How convenient he wasn't available. "Where were you?"

The first glint of the steel appeared on the edges of his smile. "Ms. Burns, you're a nurse, here on vacation with your best friend, who's been charged with my son's murder. Why would I answer that question?"

My chin lifted. "Because you're not guilty of Jeff's death."

Cregg chuckled and shook his head. "I'm guilty of many, many things. Murder isn't one of them."

I let his words sink in. He appeared forthcoming. It seemed with age came an honesty about our limitations and our faults. Cregg seemed comfortable with his.

"How do you know so much about me?" I inquired and picked at the breakfast plate.

"I don't miss much that's important to me." He crossed his legs and leaned back in the chair. "I may not have been there for Jeff like I should have been. That's the burden of parenthood. We do what we think is right and…" Cregg gave a wave of his hand. "They do what they do. But I loved my son."

Mike showed up silently, a hulking presence at my shoulder. Cregg continued. "And I'll do everything in my power to find his killer." The steely grin again. "Mike will drive you back to your car."

Speechless and chastised, I stood. Cregg had the upper hand in the conversation, and I didn't like it one bit. Mike reached for my arm, but I pulled away. "One last thing. Did you have Jeff steal the artifact?"

Cregg's eyebrows lifted. "Artifact? What are you talking about?"

I did a mental cheer. Finally, I had something over on him. "Jeff stole an artifact from the museum. It's supposed to be a fountain of youth for whoever owns it." Cregg slumped forward, and his hands gripped the chair arms. I was on to something. "Why would a healthy, virile man risk his life and freedom for that?"

"Get. Off. My. Property." Cregg never lifted his head but the anger in his voice was deadly.

Mike grabbed my arm, and I let him pull me along to an ATV. He put me in the passenger seat and buckled me in. The ride was silent down the gravel road towards the coffee farm. He stopped the vehicle behind my rental without any prompting on my part to identify the vehicle. Had they known I was here all along? And if so, how? I wasn't important enough to be spied on.

"Thanks for the fun morning." I couldn't hold my tongue as I stepped out of the ATV towards the rental car.

"Don't ever come back here again or you *and* the people you love will be sorry." The hate in his face terrified me. He gunned the engine, and gravel flew behind him as he peeled out.

Chapter Seventeen

On the drive back to the condo, my mind swirled. I'd like to blame it on too much good coffee, but it was everything that happened. Did Ashley Cregg have something to do with his son's death?

I reviewed our conversation, and my overall impression was him being honest when he said he'd did the best he could. No one got to be as successful in business as him without having a steel spine, but that didn't mean he was capable of murder. I thought back to some of the people I had known. Because someone was a success in a career didn't mean they were good or even decent parents.

Vice versa. I wondered how much he regretted about his life and if he had any peace.

My phone dinged halfway back to the resort; I ignored it to focus on the road. It was still early, and the cyclists and runners littered the shoulder. After I parked, I meandered into the serene foyer of the resort. A phone notification went off again, and I grabbed it out of my tote. Double digit missed texts and calls from Zelda.

"Oh hell," I whispered right as I ran into the shoulder of someone. My gaze flew up and apologies spilled from my mouth.

"It's okay." He turned and pushed me away.

More apologies were on my lips when I recognized him. He was the local from the beach that day on the tour.

"You…" I stared after him as he casually walked away. Koa said he vetted everyone on the tour, but it never occurred to me to consider the people on the beach that day. I followed the man through the lobby and down a hall. "Hey, wait a minute."

His pace picked up. I hurried after him. A glance over his shoulder and he took off out a side door at a run. Twenty steps outside the building and I lost him in the dense jungle-like greenery. "Well, shit." Another dead end.

The door had locked on my way out, and I walked around on a service path to the main tourist area. Zelda strode across the lawn in capris and matching tank top.

"Zelda," I called, and she turned.

"Oh, my goddess, Lexi." She threw a hip out and rested a hand on it. "Scare the living crap out of me. Can you not answer your phone?"

I approached her with my palms out. "I'm sorry. I thought if you knew where I was going you would try to stop me or worse, call Koa."

Her gaze over her sunglasses bored into me. "Uh-huh. Well," she sighed. "I guess you are in one piece. Next time at least leave a freaking note." She intertwined her arm with mine. "Let's go for breakfast."

My stomach grumbled, but not from hunger. "I've already had enough to eat." Zelda's gaze said there was no argument. "But I could have a juice."

We sat at our usual table at breakfast overlooking the beach. The juice refreshed me, and it was great to see Zelda's smile reach her eyes again. I caught her up on my morning exploits that ended with running into the surfer dude in the lobby. She listened closely, eyes huge, and stopped me a few times to ask a question.

When I finished, she leaned back and sighed. "That's a lot. What's your take on it?"

I played with the condensation on the juice glass. "I don't think Cregg was involved directly. It's just not his style."

"Makes sense," she said. "And it doesn't sound like he needed to kill Jeff so he didn't have to deal with him. He could've had the big goon you described deal with him."

I thought about that. "Maybe that's exactly what happened."

As she finished up her meal, I glanced at my phone, and I frowned. "Nothing from my parents. Have you heard from them or seen them?"

Zelda shook her head. "Nope. They seem to be spending a lot of time with that guy they stood us up for the first time we saw them at the resort. Did we ever ask who he was?"

A chill went down my spine. "No, we never did." Crap.

Zelda seemed to pick up on my anxiety. "Don't beat yourself up. We had a few things going on. Let's check their room and the beach. I'm sure they just forgot they agreed to breakfast."

In my hurry to uncover the truth and clear Zelda, I had forgotten about our breakfast plans each day with my parents. Probably the same happened with them. They got to having a good time and forgot about us. An only middle child could hope that's all it was.

After we gathered our things, we headed to my parents' room. I checked my phone again and sent them a quick text. There was no response to the text or the knock on their door.

Zelda stared at the door like she might will it to open. "Okay, this isn't great, but not horrible. Chances are they just went out, and we're making a big deal out of nothing."

I nodded. "Except the guy from the beach just happened to run into me in the lobby, and my parents just happen not be answering calls or texts."

She shrugged. "That sounds like a reach, Lex. They probably decided to go on a sunrise tour somewhere and completely forgot to let us know. We shouldn't jump to conclusions. Let's go back to the room and write down what we know." I agreed, and we turned to leave when the next-door resort guest walked out his door.

"Oh, good morning, ladies," he said as he adjusted his Hawaiian shirt, unbuttoned at his wrinkled neck. "Come to see me?"

Zelda gave him her most flirtatious smile. "We here to see Ruth and Harry Burns. Know where they ran off to?"

"No, I heard them talking on the balcony yesterday about going out on a boat." He held up his hands. "I wasn't eavesdropping, just happened to overhear. But it's been quiet over there since then."

"When did you hear them say they were going on a boat?" I asked.

"Hmmm…sometime in the afternoon. I'd just come home from pickleball and was enjoying an electrolyte beverage out on the balcony."

"Uh-huh…" As Zelda and the old man finished up their conversation, my mind wandered to my parents possibly drowning in the ocean somewhere. Zelda waved, grabbed my arm, and we walked away fast.

Back at our condo, we dropped onto the sofa. Me

numb from all the activity of the morning, and Zelda wired. "We should let the sheriff know your parents might be missing."

The feeling that something bad had happened grew into a slow fester. "Text Sam and Koa first. I trust the sheriff less."

She shrugged and punched a text into her phone. "They'll show back up, Lex. In the meantime, I'm going to the beach."

I rubbed my suddenly clammy hands on my shorts. "You go. I'm going to stay here."

She stood. "Are you sure? You won't come out for a little while?"

I shook my head. "No, I got up too early and need a nap."

"Can't argue with that. If you wake up, come on down and join me. Okay?"

I agreed and shuffled to my room. After I stretched out on the bed, I debated texting my parents again, but repeated texts wouldn't make them respond any sooner. I fell asleep and awoke to a knock at the condo front door.

Koa's handsome face filled the peephole, and a smile spread across my face as I opened the door. "You checked the peephole, right?" he asked as he entered the condo.

I inhaled the warm scent that radiated off him. "Absolutely. To what do I owe this pleasure?" I closed the door behind him.

"I thought I'd take you out for lunch. Interested?"

My lips pursed as I curled up on the sofa. "Did Zelda text you?"

He joined me on the other end of the couch. "No,

was she supposed to?"

"I think my parents are missing."

He let out a deep sigh. "Why would you think that?"

My hackles went up at his tone. "They didn't meet us for breakfast and haven't answered any calls or texts or their door when we knocked."

He nodded and ran a hand over his chin. "That is concerning. When were they last seen?"

"Yesterday afternoon, by the neighbor."

"Let's call Mikala and see if she can trace their phone." He removed the phone from the clip on his waist.

Interesting. I wondered if this was how he knew where I was so often.

He called Mikala and, after a short conversation, she said she'd call him back with the information, but it would be a while. Rather than go out for lunch, we decided to do a carryout order and bring it back to the room for us and Zelda.

****

When we returned, Zelda was still gone.

"She's probably at the beach. I'll text her." I dug through my tote, grabbed my phone, and sent her a quick text. It immediately received a like. "It's not like everyone can suddenly disappear." My nervous laugh even made me uncomfortable.

Koa took items of food out of the bags and sat them up on the table family style. "You know, you're pretty good at this investigation stuff."

I dropped into a chair and sighed. "Not by choice."

"Doesn't mean it's not a talent. This wasn't my first choice in careers either. I sort of fell into it." "

I played with the edge of the plate, resisting the urge

to pile it high with food. The scent of fried Spam, macaroni salad, and chicken katsu made my stomach grumble. "Yeah? What did you start out wanting to do?"

"I wanted to be a journalist, but there wasn't much opportunity when I was a kid." He shrugged. "So, I kind of forgot about it and went towards police work."

My hackles went up along with my walls. My ex had been a police detective. The rational part of my mind said not every police officer was like Martel, but those walls were up, nonetheless. "You were a cop?"

Koa shook his head. "During the physical exams they found a heart defect." He shrugged. "I probably would have been fine, but once my mama heard about it, that was it. My career as a police officer was over. I went to the mainland for what was supposed to be six months, turned into over twenty years. First, I worked for my uncle doing landscaping. Then I went to college and even tried law school. I did well, but not good enough. College is where I picked up investigation work on the side and went to work for the district attorney's office in San Diego."

"Then you came back here?" I felt like I had just gotten his professional resume, but nothing personal, and decided to go out on a limb. "Nothing about who you loved during that time or if you settled down." I left the door open for him to open up to me. Zelda should be back any minute, and I mentally willed her to stay away until Koa answered.

He cleared his throat. "I was married. A couple times. I have a daughter. Layla." His face lit up. "She's in college in Colorado."

"College?"

I'm old enough to have a kid in college, but it still

surprises me when friends around me did. Hell, a few of our friends from high school were grandparents. But I didn't feel old enough to have kids, much less grandkids. Somedays it feels like I just barely graduated from high school. Others, it was a thousand years ago."

Koa smiled. "She's a sophomore, studying international relations and Mandarin. I don't know where she gets her brains from."

When his phone rang, he answered it. A quick conversation with Mikala told us little. My parent's phones were powered off and unable to be traced. She said she'd keep trying, but that it did not look promising.

The door opened, and Zelda brought with her the scent of sunblock and the ocean. Her gaze traveled around the room before it settled on me. "Why do I always feel like I walked in the middle of something with you two?" She dropped her bag and towel on the floor and slid into a chair. "The food smells good." We sat awkwardly; my face flushed under their stares. "Well, come on. The food is getting cold."

We tucked into the meal and enjoyed every bite. Zelda caught us up on her day on the beach. She picked up a fair amount of gossip from the staff, but little of it was any help. Apparently, my parents had slept in separate bedrooms, My mother loved doing yoga on their balcony and both enjoyed their banana daiquiris.

"It's like they disappeared off the face of the earth," I muttered. "How is that possible?"

"People always leave a trace," Koa said. "We'll find them."

Zelda squeezed my hand. "Chances are they are out living their best life while you're sitting here getting more gray hair."

I nodded and pushed my plate aside. "I don't know, the older I get, the more separate bedrooms sound really good to me," I said, changing the subject.

Zelda dropped her fork. "Yes, please. No snoring, no hogging the covers. So much better."

After being single for so many years, sharing a bedroom with anyone wasn't appealing to me. "And you can do whatever you want without having to answer to anyone."

Silent confirmation passed between Zelda and me: our plan was genius. I glanced over at the expression of shock on Koa's face.

"I don't know what type of men you two have been with, but clearly it's not quality." He shook his head and picked up the empty plates, taking them into the small kitchen sink.

Zelda and I exchange a raised eyebrow. I couldn't help but watch him, his broad frame silhouetted against the sink as he washed the dishes. When you got to be our age, you'd be lucky not to have an entire set of baggage, even a few mismatched pieces in the back of a basement closet. Zelda started packing up the trash and ran it to the hall trash chute. I joined Koa at the sink, grabbed a towel, and dried the dishes as he washed them.

"You know, Zel and I don't hate men." I took a dish, dried it, and put it in the cabinet.

Koa's eyebrows raised. "You sure about that? Sometimes the way you two talk I wonder if you've sacrificed a few of us to some goddess in one of those cornfields in the Midwest."

"Oh no," Zelda said as she entered the kitchenette area. "We only sacrifice on the full moon. And never full-grown men; their energy is polluted. Only college boys." She gave him a wink. "Why do you think I taught high school?"

Koa's eyes grew as big as saucers.

I smacked her with the dishtowel. "Zel, that's too far."

She smiled, grabbed a water bottle from the fridge, and groaned before picking up her bag. "I'll be in my room and the patio. Don't be too noisy. Love you, but don't want to hear it." She threw a wink over her shoulder and went to her room.

Koa finished the dishes with a low whistle. "Is there anything that woman won't do?"

I chuckled and shook my head. Zelda wasn't half as daring as she talked, but cornered, she'd turned into a honey badger and rip and fight her way out. "I haven't found the line yet. Unless it involves birds. They terrify her."

"Really?" He finished the dishes and turned towards me. "That's good intel to have."

I grimaced. "I might have something to do with that. My favorite movie was that classic suspense movie with the birds swooping everywhere trying to kill people. We watched it when we were in sixth grade. I knew it wasn't real, and didn't realize she didn't." I started laughing at the image. "We were on the playground. Trying to look cool." I shook my head. "Not sure doing what, but a flock of birds came towards her, she screamed bloody murder and curled up in a ball on the blacktop." I left out the part where she peed herself.

His arms circled my waist, and his hands rubbed my back. My muscles turned to putty with each pass.

****

Sunlight, just beginning its ascent, cast a warm glow

through the leaves. Nestled against the comforting warmth behind me, I felt the cool ocean breeze dance across my skin. An arm wrapped around me, pulling me closer in a silent invitation. For the first time in what seemed like years, I was safe and secure. I inhaled deeply and sighed, content and whole and wanting this moment to go on forever. My eyes closed and drifted off again, deeply relaxed.

A jarring chime from Koa's phone shattered the perfect peace. The arm loosened; the warmth seeped away on a heavy sigh. He muttered a something under his breath as he rummaged through a pile of clothes on the floor, growing more frantic with each insistent chime.

"Koa here," he answered softly. "Yeah. Yeah." Silence turned ominous. I rolled toward him. "Shit. Where did they find the body?" He sat on the edge of the bed, in boxer briefs. The tension grew thick enough to cut with a knife. "Yeah, I know. Thanks for the heads up, bro."

The phone dropped from his ear, and his back rounded. The air hung thick with anticipation, punctuated only by the ragged gasps that escaped his lips.

I was afraid to move, frozen in place. My sense of security quickly faded. He turned to me, his face drawn. "Lex, we have a problem."

Chapter Eighteen

The air whooshed out of my body. "What now?" It couldn't get any worse. "You said body...Zelda!"

Furious, I yanked the blanket back, the sheet followed in a flurry as I kicked my legs free. Koa's hand reached out, but I swatted it away, propelled by a surge of anger. I launched myself off the bed, nearly toppling onto the carpet. "Zelda!" I screamed again.

All I could see was her body, laying on the beach, pale and lifeless, waves crashing over her. "Zel." Her name ended in a sob. Koa came off the bed and around it, squatted next to me on the floor. His arms around me as I fought to push him away. "I have to find her," I cried.

He hushed my sobs and held me close. "It's okay, Lex. It's not..."

Recent events hit me with the force of a tidal wave. "My parents. My mom. Dad..." I dissolved into full body sobs.

The bedroom door flew open, and Zelda stumbled into the room. "What in the hell?" She took two steps before the scene hit her. "Good goddess in heaven and the fields, what am I seeing?" She stood in her oversized T-shirt and panties, eyes as wide as saucers with a small kitchen knife in her hand.

I threw my arms around her and squeezed her tight. "You're alive."

"That's what I was trying to tell you," Koa growled

and pushed himself to stand.

"Is this some sort of sex plaything? I'm not judging, just curious." Zelda stared past me at Koa as he reached for his clothes.

Suddenly aware I was nude, I pulled the corner of the sheet over me. "It's nothing weird."

"Two consenting adults enjoying each other's company?" Zelda raised an eyebrow. "I can support that."

"Exactly what were you going to do with that thing?" Koa growled again as he slipped on cargo shorts.

She held the small knife up for inspection while she cocked a hip. "It might be small, but I'm confident it would have taken off your bits quite efficiently."

I dropped to the bed. "If Zelda is alive, whose body was found? Could it be my parents?" My breath came in rapid, shallow breaths.

Zelda inhaled sharply. "Someone found a body?"

Koa put his head into his cupped hands and groaned. "I received a call from a source that a body was found this morning. No early identification, but it's a male, mid-twenties. Too young for either of your parents." We gasped. "They found it out on the lava fields. It looks like it might have been…ritually posed." He mumbled the last part, hesitant.

"Pele." Zelda nodded knowingly. "The goddess is getting her revenge."

"Zelda…" I started, warning in my tone.

"This is what happens when you disrespect her." She continued, my warning unnoticed. "If Jeff hadn't taken that thing from the museum, he could still be alive, and we wouldn't be in this situation."

Koa growled deep in his chest, and I wasn't sure I

wanted to make eye contact. "Hey, do me a favor, uh? Go back to the mainland and make up stories about your own people, okay? Leave mine alone." After throwing Zelda a death stare, he stalked to the bathroom.

She dropped on the edge of the bed next to me. "I might have crossed the line there. I'm sorry."

"You did, and I'm not the one you need to apologize to."

"I will, when he comes out."

"*If* he comes out. If I were him, I'm not sure I would."

Zelda sighed. "I'm a lot first thing in the morning."

I sighed, too. "I wasn't exactly easy once I thought you were the body they found." Zelda's eyes widened. "I heard 'body' and assumed." I held my hands up. "Stupid, I know. I meet a good guy, and here I screw it up."

Koa opened the bathroom door and slipped the polo over his head. "Nah, you didn't screw anything up, Lex. You two are close, I respect that." His gaze shifted to Zelda. "Not going to lie, it's going to take me a while to get used to you. You are a lot," he said with a smile. "But have some respect for other cultures, okay?"

Zelda nodded and returned his smile. "Thanks, and I am sorry."

"Great, now that we've all made up, let me get dressed, and I'll go with you."

Koa dropped a kiss on my forehead. "I'll start the coffee." And walked out of the room.

Zelda's gaze followed as the door closed behind him. "He looks as good coming as he does going."

"He sure does," I replied on a sigh.

"Uh-huh." Zelda leaned into me and laughed. "He's a good guy?"

I nodded, blood rushed to my face.

"You didn't tell him everything that happened yesterday? At Cregg's?"

I shook my head. "No, still figuring that out."

"You two slept together?"

I shook my head. "No, but I'm still not sure why I have no clothes on…" I glanced around the room to find my pioneer nightgown on the floor.

Zelda followed my gaze and held it up. "I'm guessing you had a hot flash and stripped. If he hadn't gotten that call, you might have rocked his world." Zelda's stare examined me. "I like what I see." She rubbed my leg as she stood. "Get dressed and come outside." She stopped at the door. "If he can make good coffee, we'll need to find a way to keep him." With a wink, she disappeared out the door.

My stomach weakened. I went to the bathroom and stepped into the shower quickly. I was nothing but the flavor of the month to Koa, hell, maybe the week. Once this was over, he'd be on to the next one. That's the story I wanted to tell myself, so these feelings didn't grow and take root. But the more time I spent with him, the weaker the story became in my head.

In the mirror, my skin appeared blotchy and wrinkled, and I wondered why he was even here. Surely there were easier women out there. I dressed quickly in a tank top and stretchy shorts and cursed myself.

Koa and Zelda's laughter carried through the door. They were getting along. Any other time, it would make my heart sing, but this time it made me angrier by the second. I threw open the bedroom door to find them at the small table, enjoying coffee and laughing together.

"Lex, grab a cup. I was just telling Koa about that

time as kids we thought we saw a sniper out in the cornfield, and it ended up being a trashcan."

The memory made tears come to the corner of my eyes. My dad had gone out in the middle of the night to make sure it was a trashcan and not a sniper. If something had happened to either of them, I didn't know how the world would keep spinning. As a nurse, I had first-hand experience with death, but when it's your parents, it's a completely different thing. Something I couldn't comprehend.

Koa interrupted my thoughts "The coroner has finished, and the crime scene people are almost done. Would you believe the sheriff still hasn't shown up?" He shook his head. "The team out there is good if we want to do a quick look around."

Zelda nodded. "I'm going, too. Three heads are better than two."

I sipped the coffee and smiled. Zelda by my side, I knew we'd find my parents and all the answers.

"Sounds good." Koa glanced at me. "Ready?"

I nodded and grabbed my tote.

"Make sure to put sunblock on, and in your bag." Koa held the door open. "Don't want to get burned." I rummaged through the bag and came up with a bottle of spray sunblock.

I held it up for inspection. "Reef safe even. Good?"

Koa nodded and we left the condo for the body in the lava fields.

****

Koa's sports car hummed along the winding coastal road, its engine a low counterpoint to the rhythmic lap of waves against the shore. Outside, the Hawaiian sun cast a golden glow over the green landscape, a stark contrast to the icy tension within the vehicle. It was a serene island setting, marred by the tempest brewing in the car.

We didn't talk as Koa pulled off onto a dirt road. It became bumpier and potholes the size of the boulders threatened to swallow us.

"Don't worry, this car is low, but it can get through this."

Koa shifted gears and worked the steering wheel around the holes. We bounced in our seats until my teeth and bladder began to hurt. The road opened to a small, weathered beach, deserted of tourists and fun seekers. Police cars littered the area. Koa cut the engine, and we got out. Zelda groaned as she pulled herself out of the backseat, and I was glad I'd worn my sturdy sandals instead of fancier ones.

The sandy beach gave way to an expanse of black volcanic rock. Stunted trees with fiery red flowers dotted the stark landscape. Yellow police tape danced in the ocean breeze. My heart fluttered in my chest. Someone had died here. People walked around with cameras and other devices, doing their jobs.

A short man in dark pants and shirt approached Koa. They fist-bumped and spoke in low voices, but my attention stayed on the black rocks. Was Zelda right? Could this be the Kona curse? I shook my head and stepped closer to the men to listen.

"Bro, take a quick glance and roll. The sheriff don't want anyone out here but payroll when he shows up."

Koa nodded and patted the man on the back as he launched himself up the rocks like a spider monkey. Zelda and I followed. My muscles welcomed the stretch, but my lungs strained. It was a short, scrambled hike to the top of the crime scene.

At my side, Zelda huffed, "Whew, I need to lay off those Samuri Slings and snacks."

I attempted to even out my breathing, and not appear out of shape like I was carrying around the extra pounds. Koa wasn't fazed in the least. My hand covered my mouth. The closer to the body, the sea air mixed with the heavy scent of roasted meat gone rotten. My lungs strained.

The police tape encircled a natural indentation in the rock that was used as a fire pit. Remains of ash blew around. My stomach turned, and I coughed. "Am I breathing someone in?"

Zelda made a noise next to me. "I hesitate to ask, but I must…was the person…roasted?"

Koa shook his head. He stood with legs apart, hands on his hips, and surveyed the scene. "No, they burned some stuff there, but no human remains were found burned. Those were put on the metal stakes." A glance around showed the stakes that appeared to have been used as spikes to display something fireside. Rusted residue coated the sides, and I attempted to convince myself that's all it was, rust.

Zelda stood behind me with her eyes closed, face turned up to the sky. "I don't like this."

I nodded. "Neither do I. I don't know what ritualistic murders look like, but I'd bet money this isn't it." The area was remote, even for the island, and difficult to get to. But that doesn't mean they weren't seen by anyone. I glanced out over the ocean. The shadow of Maui was on the horizon.

Koa waved to the camera person, and we headed back down the rocks, slower this time. On the sand he turned to me, his brow furrowed. "There's nothing ritualistic about this."

Zelda's face scrunched. "The vibes are off."

Koa shrugged. "Of course they are. Someone died violently here. We've got to head back. Sheriff Martel is on his way; we should be gone before he gets here."

We piled into the car. Conversation was stunted as I tried to not bite my lip or bounce out of the car. Once back on the main road, I breathed a sigh of relief.

Front the back seat, Zelda groaned. "Why the fire if they didn't burn the body? Especially since the fire might be seen from the main road at night."

Koa's hand tightened on the steering wheel. "Evidence. Enough to connect the murderer to the crime. Or to another crime—possibly the murder of one Jeff Parks."

My eyes squeezed shut as I pushed down the urge to throw up. "Do we know that for sure?"

Koa rolled his eyes. "Okay, what are the chances the island's homicide rate skyrockets, and they aren't connected, *and* we're not involved? It's too much to ask."

"There was enough of a head for an ID?" Zelda asked, her own head now between the front seats.

His hand tightened on the steering wheel. "They could still ID the remains. Shane Lincoln."

"Ah, crap." I twisted in my seat to lock gazes with Zelda.

"Does that name mean something?" he inquired.

Zelda licked her lips and leaned back in the seat. "Only the supposed witness to me committing murder."

"Right." Koa's deadpan tone caused my hackles to go up. Did he forget that, or did that fact miss him?

I shuddered, unable to think about what Shane could

have done to deserve a death like that. I dug into my tote for my phone and searched for Shane Lincoln. Top of the search was social media pages featuring a smiling young man with tanned skin and sun-bleached hair.

"Well, hell." I held the phone over my shoulder for Zelda. She repeated my curse.

Koa frowned. "What now?"

I slide through pictures and sites. "Shane just happens to have been at the resort the same morning I came back from Cregg's. I ran into him in the lobby. I thought I recognized him and tried to follow but lost him through an employee entrance."

Zelda huffed. "I can tell you why. He's not only the dude from the beach, but also a server at the resort lounge. Remember the other day when I said I thought I recognized someone?"

The pieces of the puzzle clicked together. Shane was the missing piece in all of this. But there were still unanswered questions. How did a random surfer dude factor into a murder and artifact theft? And get himself killed in the process? "Are you sure, Zelda? Like one hundred percent sure?"

She nodded. "I remember seeing him when we went to the lounge together but thought he just looked familiar, you know? Like someone I knew that looked like him, but not him. But I'm sure now. He was in the lounge the night Jeff was killed."

Koa's jaw clenched. "That's why eyewitnesses are rarely right."

Zelda huffed. "Are you saying I'm lying?"

"No, I'm saying it's possible you're misremembering." Koa maneuvered the car around between black rock and a crater.

She crossed her arms with a huff. Her own experience said he was right, but she was stubborn enough to know she was right, too. "He looked familiar before and definitely does now."

I stopped strolling on group photos of Shane at a cookout and zoomed in. "Koa, you say you are familiar with everyone. How come you don't recognize him?"

"Yeah, you work at the resort, but you don't recognize him?" Zelda added, her tone forceful.

The tension rolled off Koa in waves. "Do you know how many people work at the resort? Hundreds. I've been away from the island for years. This guy wasn't even born when I left. I might know his parents, but not every single person."

"Hmmm...." The fact he didn't say yes, or no, wasn't lost on me. And it seemed convenient he knew people sometimes and not others. As it was, I wasn't buying it. Soon enough, we were back at the resort.

Koa parked in the circle drive and moved to get out. I reached for his arm and gave it a squeeze. "I think I'm going to go to the sheriff's office about my parents." He opened his mouth to protest, and I held up my hand. "I get it, but it's been long enough without hearing from them, and it's not right. For all I know, they could have a health emergency somewhere. The authorities need to be notified."

"If that's what you want to do, I'll go with you."

I shook my head. "Best I do this on my own. Even Zelda going with me would cause a ruckus. I appreciate it, though." I patted his arm and pulled myself out of the car. Zelda followed.

We threw big smiles and waves at Koa as he drove away. I wrapped my arm through Zelda's and crossed through the lobby to breakfast. "I thought you were going to the police," she said.

I shook my head. "No, at least not with Koa, and not right now. I'm not sure he's a part of this."

"Does this mean I'm in the clear with you?" Zelda asked.

"Oh yeah, no way you could have cut up that body and done all of that on those black rocks."

"Whew, finally."

I pursed my lips. "You knew I didn't trust you fully?"

Zelda threw back her head and laughed. "Girl, I sense when you're constipated. Of course, I knew you still didn't trust me. But I realized it would work out." She winked and laughed harder. "See what I did there?"

I joined in, glad to have a light moment. But it wouldn't last.

Chapter Nineteen

We had just sat down and ordered when my phone dinged. I dug it out of my tote to see a text from my mom. "Hmm…"

"What?" Zelda sipped her juice. "Mr. Stache is on his way back? Can't get enough of you?"

"It's a text from my mom."

I turned the phone to Zelda so she could read the screen. —*Hey Lexi! Sorry, it's been a minute since we talked. We're just having the time of our lives. Don't worry about us! See you soon! XOXO*—

She lifted her sunglasses to read the text. "No way that's your mom."

I stared at the phone. "It doesn't even sound like her. They haven't had the time of their lives in decades."

"Someone has her phone." The server put the plates down and Zelda dug into her scrambled eggs and bacon.

I didn't want to eat, but I had to keep my energy up. I picked at the French toast and sausage.

"If they have her phone, they have her." My fork clanged on the plate as the realization hit me. "Or did, before they burned her body or threw it in the ocean…" The words caught in my throat.

Zelda reached for my arm. "Lex…" She was cut off when her attention was drawn to the security dude in a fuchsia shirt marching towards us. Keawe's slim chest puffed out as he spoke. "Ma'am, would you come with me?"

"For what?" I crossed my arms. "Where?"

He threw a side eye at me. "That's no concern of yours."

Other guests had noticed the scene at our table.

"But it is," I said. "My friend and I were enjoying a nice breakfast, and you interrupted it with a demand."

He rested his hands on his hips. "I'd like to speak with Zelda for a moment."

She shook her head. "No, thanks." And absently picked up her fork.

He took a step forward and leaned on the table with his fingers spread out. "That wasn't really a request, ladies. It's either me or the sheriff."

I rolled my eyes. "Can we do this privately? There are cameras all over this place. You won't miss us." I huffed loudly and adjusted the napkin on my lap. "At least let us finish breakfast."

His stare flittered between us before he barely nodded. "Fine, but if it's one minute after you finish breakfast or either of you try anything, the full force of the sheriff's office will be on top of you. And I mean on top of you. They will run you down and cause a scene you can't imagine."

Zelda held up her hands. "Okay, okay." He stalked away like he had a stick up his butt. "So, what are we going to do?"

I took a sip of the coffee and checked over each shoulder for anyone listening in before I answered. "We're going on the run."

Zelda sniffed. "Wish I'd taken a shower."

I suppressed a smile. "You're fine. That deodorant is really holding up to the seventy-two hours promise on those commercials. We've got to find out who killed the surfer kid, and Jeff, and find my parents."

She nodded and popped the last of the toast in her mouth. "That's a lot. Luckily, it's all connected."

"And we can't be hung up by stupid hotel security or sheriffs or shady men."

"Agreed. But how do we get out of here?"

I leaned back in the chair like I didn't have a care in the world and stretched. I hadn't been sure cameras were everywhere until Keawe confirmed it. But that was most likely only in public areas. The resort wouldn't waste the money watching employees take out the trash or go for a smoke. At least that's what I was counting on. "We'll head towards the front desk in a few minutes. Make it look like we're complying. Then make a run for it through the service exit. We'll circle back to the car and be off." At least I hoped that's how it went.

Zelda blew out a breath. "You get I'm not a runner, right? I know you did track in high school, but that was one season, and I think you tore your calf muscle? Like, running isn't our strength here, Lex. Got anything else?"

"Ha, no. That's all I got. We don't have to run. In fact, the slower we go, the better." I remembered back to the overgrown paths. "The other day when I was following Shane, I took the employee paths. They're not maintained, and we can easily hide. The quieter we are, the harder it'll be to find us."

"Okay, I can go slow."

We moved the food around on our plates for a few more minutes before deciding it was time.

"Let's do it." I stood and threw my tote over my shoulder. The weight of the artifact a reminder of what was at stake. We exited the restaurant and headed for the lobby. "Ready?"

Zelda answered with a nod. I grabbed her hand, and we made a beeline for the service door. Our feet hit the cracked pavement, and we took off at a brisk walk. The thick greenery hit our shoulders as we passed. My ears strained to listen for footfalls of pursuit.

"Breathe," Zelda whispered loudly over my shoulder, and I inhaled. We were halfway to the parking lot when a door slammed, and the sounds of a ruckus came from behind. I dragged her into the bushes where we hid behind.

Martel and Keawe flew by, radios squawking, and belts jingling. Zelda and I stayed in place in the bushes, our foreheads together. When things quieted, Zelda separated from me. She took a step backwards when the rattle of keys and belts returned, along with the men struggling to catch their breath.

Martel sauntered by, hands resting on his gun belt. "You said you had this under control."

Keawe brought up the rear. "I did. How did they realize there are no cameras out here? Those two are smarter than they look." He shook his head. "You should have just come in and arrested them. Hell, you should have done that days ago, before they put it together." He huffed out another breath. "Damn it, if it wasn't for those two, we wouldn't have had to get rid of Shane."

Martel stopped directly in front of the spot where we were hiding. The breath froze in my chest; I tightened my arm that held the tote containing the artifact against my chest. Zelda moved to her hand to her bag, and I stilled her with a shake of my head. Her little knife might cut a finger off, but it would be no match for these two men with guns.

He threw his hands in the air. "You're giving these broads way more credit than they deserve. We'll find them and get this settled." He dropped his hands on the security guard's shoulders and massaged them gently. "Before you know it, we'll be rolling in dough and done with this menial crap, okay?" Keawe didn't meet Martel's gaze. "Okay, babe?"

Keawe turned to face him. "Fine, just make sure you get them for this and find the damn artifact. Housekeeping has searched their room and still hasn't found it. We need that money."

Their lips met in a tender, passionate embrace, their bodies drawn close as they shared a moment of intimate connection.

Zelda and my eyes met wide, wide as dinner plates. Not only did these two men work together, but they were a couple. Interesting. Another thing Koa never mentioned, and he claimed to know everyone.

Martel gently cupped Keawe's cheek. "Before you know it, we'll be on our own boat, sailing into the sunset. Just you and me and not a care in the world."

The two separated and headed back to the main building. I counted to one hundred before I motioned for Zelda to follow.

"Did I just have a stroke, or did those two just admit to murder? Multiple times?" Zelda stage whispered next to me.

I held a finger to my lips to silence her. Back on the path, we moved slowly, ready to jump back into the overgrowth anytime. The car sat unattended in the parking lot, and we made a jog for it, jumped in, and slammed the doors. My hands shook as the engine turned over, and I threw it into reverse out of the parking space and drove away slowly so as not to draw attention.

When our wheels hit the blacktop of the highway, we exhaled, and a line of expletives came out of Zelda. "What in the creation was that?" She glanced behind us. "Am I being arrested again? Just you? Both of us? They're a couple? I'm so confused."

I looked back, but no flashing lights followed us. We had gotten away for now. "I don't know. But Martel and Keawe are the ones framing you, that's for certain. Or both of us?" My head spun. I let out a nervous laugh. If I heard a patient make that laugh, I'd check the chart for psych meds and put in a request to up the dosage.

Zelda flopped against the seat and held a hand to her forehead. "Where are we going that Martel can't get us? Off the island? Is that even possible?"

My mind raised, and I remembered what Martel had said when we first crossed paths. "We're in one of the most isolated places in the world."

Zelda snorted. "Ha, paradise."

Chapter Twenty

As my hands flexed on the steering wheel, I saw that my knuckles had gone white. "Even if we did get off the island, and that was a big *if*, there's nowhere to go."

It was Zelda's turn for the crazy cackle.

I slammed my hand on the steering wheel, and she jumped. "I've got it. We go to Cregg."

"What? Like the billionaire? Did you two hit it off that well?" She stared at me incredulously. "I thought he had you escorted off his property."

"He did. But I have a feeling that's where we're supposed to be."

Zelda shrugged and closed her eyes. "Fine, wake me up when we get there. I'm a morning person, but this is all too much."

I couldn't agree more and focused my attention on the road. It didn't take long to find the turnoff to the coffee farm. Instead of stopping at the farm, I continued up the gravel road I remembered Mike used to bring me back to my car. I drove slowly and parked in front of the hulking mansion. I reached over and smacked Zelda awake.

"We're here."

She leaned forward and stared through the windshield. "Is this Cregg single?"

I thought back to the wispy white hair and liver-spotted hands. "Don't even go there. Let's move." I opened the car door, which was immediately grabbed by Cregg's private security guard. "Hey Mike, you talking today?"

His grim expression gave nothing away. We stared at each other until he waved a hand for us to get out of the car. I grunted and moved to stand. "Is Mr. Cregg home?" He ignored me and herded us toward the house.

Zelda took in Mike's bulging muscles beneath the tight T-shirt and camo cargo pants. "What is it with these dudes wearing clothes that shrunk in the dryer? Not that I'm complaining." She leaned into me. "Is he single?"

I shook my head in warning as we walked up the steps into the house. With a breezy gesture, Mike ushered us into a cozy living room that flowed seamlessly onto a patio overlooking the vast ocean. "Have a seat here. Mr. Cregg is out on the boat and due back soon. I'll have the staff bring refreshments." With that, he left the room.

My eyebrow raised. He could speak complete sentences. Moments later, the same woman as my last visit appeared, tray in hands. It was ladled with pastries, breads, fruit, and cheeses. Juice and water finished off the offerings. With a smile, she left the room.

I poured myself and Zelda glasses of water, and sat back against the plush chair. Zelda reached for a pastry.

"No, girl. We don't need that on top of everything else." Chastised, she picked up the water glass and drank, but not before she stuck her tongue out. Cregg's staff had left us alone, and the silence of the room was oddly comforting. I finished the water and had started to relax when a boat appeared at the dock outside.

I stood and stepped onto the patio. Zelda followed. Cregg jumped off the boat onto the dock like a man half his age, as staff grabbed ropes and tied the boat up. Mike met him on the dock. They exchanged words. Behind them, an employee extended a short plank for the two people who stood on the side of the boat. One of them laughed and, even with someone holding their hand, almost fell into the water. As they walked down the plank, it hit me who they were.

"Mom!" I screamed and ran across the lawn as fast as my middle-aged legs would carry me. "Dad!" I didn't care if Mike knocked me to the ground or even shot me. I hit the dock, and my parents had their arms out, waiting for me. I threw my arms around them and squeezed as hard as I could. "You're okay," I repeated over and over.

"There, there, girl. We're fine." Dad ran a hand over my hair. I pulled away and wiped the tears and snot from my face with my arm.

Mom stared at me as if I'd grown a second head. "Alexandra. What has gotten into you? We're fine. I almost fell into the water over there, but that nice gentleman grabbed my arm in time."

"We thought something happened to you." Zelda was behind me, her voice broke with emotion.

Mom huffed. "Why ever would you think something like that?"

I shook my head, speechless. Here in the sunlight by the ocean, everything, Zelda being accused of murder, dead bodies all over the place, even the image of my parents dead somewhere, all seemed to be a bad dream.

Cregg cleared his throat behind us. "Let's head to the house. Vana has refreshments set out for us." He floated past us.

Dad did a jig and moved fast to catch up with Cregg. "Did she make more of her lilikoi mochi?" Cregg

161

laughed and patted Dad on the back. I stared after them as the two men walked to the house.

"Come on, before the boys eat all the good stuff." Mom wrapped an arm around me and Zelda and led us back to the house.

As Zelda and I followed Mom across the perfect lawn to the mansion, I whispered, "I think Cregg is keeping them hostage."

Her eyes widened. "Who? Your parents?" She glanced at them. "I don't think so, Lex. They seem fine. I don't think I've seen them this happy since…you broke up with that one loser in high school. They were just out on a boat, for heaven's sake."

I waved a hand in their direction. "Exactly. What better way to hold someone against their will than to make them think it was their decision?"

Zelda stopped and turned to me. "Okay, Lexi. No. That's way more work than Cregg needs to do. He could throw them in a dungeon somewhere and be done with it. Or push them off the side of the boat in the middle of the ocean." She rested a hand on my shoulder. "Let's see where this goes, okay?" She gave me a squeeze and dragged me towards the house. "It's odd, I'll give you that. But the feeling I'm getting is good."

Staff bustled about, setting up drinks and snacks. Dad and Cregg found chairs and drinks and were enjoying both when we stepped onto the patio. Dad lifted a glass in a mock salute to us. "Girls, grab a drink. Mom is in the bathroom."

We chose glasses filled with something bright pink with bits of fruit on top. One sip refreshed and cooled me. With a sigh, I took a familiar seat near the men as Zelda picked through the snack choices.

I figured no time to waste to get to the truth. "I didn't know you all knew each other."

Cregg smiled wanly. "We met at the airport when your parents arrived. I haven't had so much fun in years as I've had with Ruth and Harry here."

Dad nodded and bit into a light pink round confection. "Same, Ash, same. We've really enjoyed you and your hospitality. You'll have to come to Florida and visit us sometime."

Cregg and Dad clicked their glasses. Moisture on the outside flew. "I do love Florida," he said.

"Well then, you're in for a treat. Our Ch—"

"Whew, did ya'll leave anything for me?" Mom floated out of the house; the fabric of her tropical print muumuu flowed behind her.

Cregg threw her a glance over his shoulder. "Always leave more than enough for a beautiful lady."

I took in the vibe between them. It was friendly and comfortable. Friends who enjoyed each other. Maybe Zelda was right, and I was paranoid.

Zelda plopped down next to me with a full plate of fruit, mochi, cheeses, and meat. I groaned silently. This was her third breakfast of the morning.

"Mr. Cregg, I must ask. Did you know Harry and Ruth were my parents when you befriended them?"

Cregg didn't hesitate. "Not at all. I only found out after you left here the other day. Ruthie mentioned they missed breakfast with you all, and I had one of the staff text you for her."

I scoffed. "You had staff text me? Really?"

Dad waved a hand at me. "When I say Ashley here has taken care of everything, Lexi, I mean it. No one's wiping our butts, but otherwise, everything."

"So, there is a limit to what money can do," Zelda interjected next to me.

I gave her a side eye and resisted the urge to smack her.

Cregg set his glass down and casually rested his hands on his stomach. "Lexi, I'm used to having staff take care of everything for me." He shrugged. "It didn't occur to me that with you and Zelda's situation, it would be viewed as anything other than helpful."

I nodded and sipped the drink. The truth was straightforward, and I believed him, even if it was weird.

"Must be nice," Zelda said around a mouthful of mochi.

Ashley favored her with a smile. "It's a nice problem to have. One of many I've had for too long and accept as normal."

Zelda cleared her throat. "So, Sheriff Martel and Keawe, the head of security at your hotel are framing me for your son's murder. You know anything about that?"

Cregg's brows knitted together. "They also murdered their one accomplice, Shane Lincoln. But yes, I do know something about that. I know everything." He glanced around the group at our drinks. "You'll want to refill your drinks before I get started."

Dad heaved a sigh and stood. "I'll need a snack for energy. I have no idea what's happening, but I need to keep my blood sugar levels up."

We waited for Dad to fill a plate and retake his seat before Cregg continued.

"Martel and Jeff knew each other since they were kids. Jeff's mom would bring him here every summer to visit me. They were as thick as pea soup."

"Like you and Zelda, honey," Mom interjected.

I huffed. Zelda and I never committed murder, so not exactly like us. But we still had time. "When you said Jeff had contacted you, he was on the island. He wasn't here just to say 'hi' was he?"

Cregg sat quietly for so long the only sound was Dad and Zelda chomping on food. I was about to repeat the question when he finally answered.

"I mentioned a curse earlier. Money can be a curse. So can all that comes with it. It was for Jeff and my relationship. I thought I'd found solace here on the island. Peace. I thought buying land would help the local population and control inflation. Stop other developers with worse intentions buying it all up and pricing the locals out." He held his hands out. "But that wasn't the case. I didn't make my money in real estate. I should have stayed out of it."

Mom reached for Cregg's shoulder and rubbed it gently. "Ashley, honey. Take your time."

He nodded and rested a hand on Mom's, squeezing it. "Thanks, Ruthie. You see, girls, ever since I came here, I've felt at home, but things don't work out. I try to help, and it blows up, every single time. And now...I've also been diagnosed with pancreatic cancer."

My breath froze in my throat. Pancreatic cancer is almost always fatal. Treatment could work if caught early enough, but I'd wager Cregg's wasn't. "Eternal youth," I whispered.

Cregg's smile was sad, and he wiped a hand across his eyes. "Jeff texted the day he died and said he had a cure. I thought it would be something a quack gave him, or he read about. Some ointment or device that will cure everything. Even after Martel came here to notify me, I didn't put it together. It wasn't until the news of the stolen artifact hit the papers that I put it together."

Silence fell over the patio. Cregg had lost a son and would soon lose his life to cancer. No amount of money or success would or had stopped any of it. It all seemed tragic.

Mom sniffed. "Jeff risked everything for you to be healed."

"Not exactly, Mom." I interjected. "Jeff had a gambling problem and was in significant debt. The trust had recently run out. He was looking for another meal ticket."

Cregg nodded. "All part of the curse, it seems."

Mom tilted her head up and stared me down through her glasses. "Well, thankfully we're poor, so don't be getting any ideas, Alexandra."

Dad muttered a curse. "We're not poor, we're frugal."

I held up a hand. "Either way, I'm not committing a crime for either of you, so you're fine."

Zelda cleared her throat. "Why would Martel and Keawe kill Jeff? Why not just let him bring you the artifact?"

Cregg took a sip of his drink. "Martel has been like a son to me for years. Even when Jeff would visit, it was more like a son having a friend visit."

"Martel wanted the credit for healing you. He didn't want Jeff to take any of the limelight away from him."

"Or money," Zelda added.

Cregg nodded. "Keawe also has something in common with Jeff. They both have a gambling problem."

Zelda sat her plate aside and sighed loudly. "That's all well and good, but how am I going to get out of murder charges?"

"Lexi, bubala, weren't you going to work on that?" Mom asked, her head down in disapproval. A stare I was familiar with from the rare occurrence of bringing a "B" home on a report card.

Cregg chuckled softly. "That's the reason she came here, wasn't it?" He stared at me like he could see through me. I didn't like the feeling. "She knew I was the key and came to unlock the mystery."

I kicked the tote with my foot to remind myself the artifact was still there. The heaviness of it reassured me as I spoke. "You'll go to the FBI and get them involved? Clear Zelda?" I wasn't sure who if anyone was over Sheriff Martel on the island, but figured the FBI was over everyone.

Cregg nodded. "Absolutely. No reason for more lives to be destroyed needlessly." He patted his thighs. "Now that we have that settled, how about we retire to the house for a nap? Maybe you call that boyfriend of yours and have him meet you here?"

"Boyfriend?" Mom asked. All eyes turned on me.

"Koa." Cregg's eyebrow arched. "You didn't think he and Sam just happened to show up in your lives, did you?"

"You really are the key to all of this?" I leaned back in the chair, exhausted. "Everything has been some little game to you."

"Bubala," my mother said, "I don't fully understand half of what is happening here, but I know Ashley is a good, honest man. And you and Zelda are good women. Whatever happened, the bad doesn't involve him."

Cregg shook his head. "Thank you, but that's not totally true, Ruth. Sam has been on my payroll long before any of this. He has run interference between myself and the locals when I've messed up more times than I can count. Invaluable. Koa, was another matter."

Zelda cleared her throat. "Koa wasn't hired to watch us or befriend us?"

"Not at all. If I didn't know better, I'd think he was putting a curse on me. He works with Sam sometimes, but not for me. This was an exception."

I pursed my lips. Was this the odd feeling I had with Koa that made me keep him at a distance? He said they took the occasional job but had expressed anger at Cregg. It was possible he worked for Cregg and still didn't like him. Hell, half the people I knew didn't like their employers or bosses, that was nothing new. Still, it didn't reconcile my feelings with Koa.

It was just then Koa strutted in. Tan shorts tight and polo strained. My breath caught and my emotions were on a rollercoaster. He didn't look at me but went straight to Cregg.

"Sir." Koa's voice was clipped and professional. "Martel and Keawe are headed this way. They were able to pick up the ankle bracelet signal. What would you like me to do?"

Cregg glanced over his shoulder at Koa, a look of consternation on his face.

I spoke up. "We can't be found here." I reached down and touched the artifact in the tote. A plan formed in my mind. "Get the ankle bracelet off Zel. We'll throw it in the bushes over there." I pointed in the direction I came through from the coffee farm a few days prior. "Can you get us back to the resort without anyone knowing?" I asked Koa.

He looked at me for the first time. "We can go through the beach after dark. We'll use Cregg's boat. I'll drive the rental down to the farm and leave it there. It'll look like you two disappeared from there."

I nodded. "Perfect. They'll find the ankle bracelet in the brushes and will have no reason to search the house. We'll stay there until dark. Mr. Cregg, call the FBI. We're going to get both of those men to admit to the murder of not only your son, but Shane Lincoln as well."

Chapter Twenty-One

Around me, a chorus of voices rose in protest. I slowly pushed myself to a standing position, legs apart, hands on both hips. "No, this is happening. I'm putting an end to this tonight."

Zelda popped up next to me. "I can't let you do that, Lex. I'm the one that got us into this, that did everything. I should be the one to do it."

Dad leaned forward, his hands resting on his thighs. "Neither of you should be doing this. Ash, Koa, can't you just arrest these two *eejits* and call it a day?"

Koa rubbed his chin. "Right now, we have nothing but theory and hearsay on either of them. Especially since they killed their accomplice. We need a confession. Especially since they are both law enforcement."

Zelda sunk back into the chair. "Shane? The surfer dude was their accomplice?"

Koa nodded.

My head dropped. "Martel knew Jeff was stealing the artifact and sent him to get it at the beach, but something went wrong."

"Very wrong," Zelda said sarcastically. "Let's do it." She stared up at me. "Or you do it." She shrugged. "I'll be by your side either way."

I reached for her hand and squeezed it.

Mom moved to the edge of her seat. "Ash, honey. I hesitate to ask, but...couldn't you just...create the

170

confession? I don't want the girls in danger."

Cregg's lips trembled, and he wiped a hand across them absently. "I could, but I won't. I wouldn't be the person you think I am if I did."

Mom nodded and fell back into the chair as she chewed on her cheek. My opinion of Ashley Cregg went up a thousand points. I dug my phone out of my tote and texted Keawe.

—*Sorry we ran out. We're ready to turn ourselves in this evening. Meet you in our condo at eight tonight.*—

Keawe responded immediately. —*Okay*—

Koa moved beside my mother. "Don't worry, Mrs. Burns. I'll make sure she's safe." Mom nodded in his direction but didn't speak. Worry etched her wrinkled brow.

Cregg's quiet voice ended the conversation. "I'll take you girls back this evening. Get some rest between now and then."

A heavy silence fell over the group. The waves and sunshine seemed too shiny and out of place. The housekeeper walked Zelda and me to a guest room. It featured two queen beds with Hawaiian quilts and a connected bathroom that was bigger than my bedroom back home.

We took turns in the shower and collapsed onto the beds. The sheets were cool and soft against our skin. We were drifting off to sleep when a soft knock came at the door.

It opened to Koa, peeking his head in. "Hey." He held up a paper bag. "I picked up a few clothes and things for you both. Figured you'd want a change of clothes."

I snuggled deeper into the bed. "Thanks, you can put them on over there." I pointed to the dresser. The artifact was tucked into one of the drawers, and I wasn't ready for him to find it. He placed the bag there and stared at us for a moment. His hands moved back and forth on his sides like he was waving something off himself.

"I want you to know I helped you because I wanted to. Cregg doesn't own me. I want you to know that."

I nodded, unsure of what to say. His statement had a lot to unpack, and now wasn't the time. He stared for a moment longer, nodded, and closed the door behind himself.

"See, I told you he likes you." Zelda punched the pillow and rolled away from me.

I smiled. She was right.

****

I didn't think I would be able to sleep, but when I woke up, the room was dark, and Zelda sat on the other bed dressed in a grey T-shirt and black capris leggings Koa had brought from the condo. A tray of food and a pitcher of water sat in front of her. I groaned and pushed the covers back.

"Good morning, sunshine. Or should I say good evening?" she said, with a vampire accent on the last words. I took the glass she poured me gratefully. The water washed the last of sleep from me, and I was wide awake. "You ready for tonight?" I nodded and popped a piece of mango into my mouth. "Great, because I'm coming with you." Before I could protest, she shook her head. "I'm not doing this because I feel guilty. I'm doing this because I'm not letting you do this alone. You'd probably rather have Mr. Stache, but you're getting me."

I chewed and thought. There was no reason to fight with Zelda once she got an idea in her head. Koa most likely had more experience doing such things, but Zelda had more heart and spunk. "I couldn't imagine doing it without you. We're always better together, anyway."

Her smile lit up the room. "Exactly. They have dinner downstairs for us whenever we head down there."

I chugged the water and grabbed a piece of pineapple before I slid out of the bed. "Let me get dressed and head down. I'd rather get this over with before my anxiety takes a couple of years off my life, and I change my mind."

Zelda swung her legs off the bed and opened the paper bag Koa left earlier. She dumped it on the bed and dug through the clothes. "Not bad. It's like he knows us."

She threw black leggings and a T-shirt my way, with fresh undies. I put them on and shoved the thought of Koa touching my panties out of my head. That was as close as he would get to them. Although, even as I said it to myself, I knew it was a full-on lie. Now wasn't the time, but I had fallen for him. Completely and more thoroughly than I had done since I could remember.

Dressed, we headed downstairs. Late afternoon sun filtered through the dining-room windows. Koa rested his arms on the table in deep conversation with Cregg. The conversation stopped when we entered.

"Don't stop on our account," I said and dropped into a chair.

Koa sighed. "We were debating whether Cregg would pilot the boat this evening."

My eyebrow rose.

"Koa hasn't been out on the waters in years. I'm out on them almost daily and can sail to the resort with my eyes closed."

Zelda grunted next to me. "Seems like you'd have staff to take care of that?"

Cregg chuckled. "I pay people to do the things I don't want to do, but I love the ocean. If I hadn't gone into tech, I would have been a sailor."

I took in his now fragile state and wondered what he was like in his youth. "Can't blame you there. Koa, let Cregg help. He's an adult and knows what he is capable of."

Koa stared at me a long time before he nodded.

My face warmed, and I hoped in the dim light of the dining room no one would notice. "Did Martel and Keawe buy our disappearance story?" I inquired.

Cregg's fingers tapped on the table. "They didn't even come to the main house. Mike handled everything. Occasionally, I do something right, like hire good people."

"Now, we were promised dinner before we take down local law enforcement."

Cregg gracefully stood and gave us a bow. "Of course, ladies. One moment." He disappeared and returned with a large platter laden with grilled meats, roasted potatoes, and fresh fruit. We piled our plates high and enjoyed every bite. I resisted myself not to eat too much. The last thing I wanted was to have a full stomach and be running around.

It was agreed Koa would not travel with us. The boat would consist of Cregg, myself, and Zelda. The walk to the boat was solemn and had an air of finality to it. Like we might not come this way again. I wasn't sure how I felt about that.

Chapter Twenty-Two

Ashley Cregg expertly piloted the boat through the black waves. As the boat rocked, my stomach rolled with the motion. I was glad I hadn't overindulged in dinner. As it was, I struggled to hold on to what I had ate. I gripped the side of the boat and watched the lights of the resort grow brighter as we approached.

Full darkness had descended on the resort. Few people walked the beach, and none on the dock. Strains of music drifted from the resort lounge, and the occasional cheer carried on the wind.

Cregg guided the boat to the dock. "All right, ladies, I'll be seeing you."

Zelda gave him a side eye. "Are you sure about that?"

He gave us a genuine smile and patted each of us on the shoulder as we stepped onto the dock. "Yes, ma'am. I'll be seeing more of both of you."

Something about the firm pat on the shoulder gave me optimism that all of this would work out. I returned his smile and a wave as we walked towards the resort.

Zelda and I didn't pass anyone as we walked through the moonlight grounds to our building and took the elevator to the condo. Inside, everything appeared the same.

She turned in a circle. "Is this place somehow cleaner than when we left?"

I glanced around the room. "Seems the same. But I would bet good money housekeeping and maybe even security gave it a very thorough cleaning while we were gone."

She shrugged. "I guess wishful thinking. How much time until Martel gets here?"

My stomach rolled, and I glanced at my phone. "We've got fifteen minutes."

"Great." With a groan and an enormous sigh, Zelda dropped onto the couch. "Fifteen minutes of dread and tension. Fantastic."

I joined her. "It's like waiting for a hot date."

Zelda laughed and closed her eyes. "Remember when we were younger, and every date was hot?"

I joined her, laughing. "Okay, I don't remember all of them being hot."

"Maybe not all of them, but they seem that way in hindsight," she admitted with a sigh. "Things always seem better in retrospect."

I couldn't disagree. Since leaving my previous nursing job, I'd forgotten the stress of understaffed shifts and the stupidity of administration and only remembered working with patients and good coworkers.

Though that could be chalked up to dehydration.

We were reminiscing about the past when a knock at the door silenced our conversation. Zelda pulled her cell phone from her pocket, turned on the recorder, and set it face down on the end table next to the couch. It seemed like it took us forever to stand and cover the few steps to the condo door. My hand rested on the doorknob, and I turned to face Zelda, the blood drained from her face and lips tight. I gave a small nod, and she returned it. With those small gestures, I opened the door.

Martel and Keawe stood in the doorway; both wore looks of resigned annoyance. Like our mere existence had put them out. When you consider everything, it kind of did.

"Evening." I held the door open for them to enter and hoped my voice was stronger than I felt. They sauntered in. Keawe's head twisted side to side as he took in the space. Martel moved immediately to check out the bedrooms. They trusted us as much as we trusted them. Good to be clear on that.

After I closed the door, Zelda and I retook our positions on the couch. I reached for her hand, and she squeezed mine back. Years of friendship, pain, and occasional stupidity made us smarter women. We had this.

Martel and Keawe moved chairs from the dining table and placed them in front of us. Nervous energy radiated off Keawe; I wondered if the same could be said of Zelda and me. I took a deep breath and pushed it down. They might be professional law enforcement as well as evil criminals, but we were middle-aged women. I'd put money on me and Zelda in a fight.

Martel cleared his throat. "You said you have information about the case." He motioned with his hands for us to speak. "Are you finally doing the right thing and turning yourselves in?"

I squeezed Zelda's hand. "Yes, no." As I cleared my throat, it tightened involuntarily. I forced myself to relax in order to speak. "We heard about Shane Lincoln's death."

Keawe's sneaker bounced on the floor. "Would you know anything about that?"

Martel barked a laugh. "Ladies, this isn't how it

goes. You have information. You tell us what you know. That's how this works."

Zelda crossed her legs and gave a dramatic sighed. "Well, we found the artifact. Figured we need to turn it over to you all."

Keawe bounced to the edge of the chair, legs tense at the mention of the artifact. "You have it? Here?"

I crossed my arms to mimic Zelda's body language. "We didn't say that."

Martel shook his head. "Ladies—"

Zelda interrupted him. "Stop with the *ladies* BS, Martel. We have the artifact. You want the artifact. And we're going to tell you what you're going to do to get it."

I tried not to stare at her. She sounded for all the world like a detective from the black-and-white movies we used to stay up late in middle school watching during sleepovers. Laughter threatened to bubble over at the craziness of the situation, but I coughed it down.

Keawe's fists balled on his thighs. "Where is it?" Weighted silence filled the room. "Where. Is. The. Artifact?" He spat out the words, each one its own sentence, jaws clenched so tight his jowls vibrated.

Martel reached out one a hand and covered Keawe's fist. "We are willing to negotiate. But we'll need to see the artifact first."

"No go, buckaroo," Zelda said. I was amazed at how calm she appeared. "How about this? We tell you what we want, and you give it to us. Then you get the artifact."

I counted to ten and jumped in. "We want all charges against Zelda dropped. And any against me. Both of us are cleared of any wrongdoing."

Keawe glanced at Martel, then groaned. "Why would we do that when you both committed crimes?"

Zelda shook her head. "Oh, come on. You know we didn't do it."

Martel's eye raised. "How do we know that? There's an eyewitness and—"

My heart wouldn't survive much more of this tension. I was tired of the game playing and wanted it to end. "Screw the eyewitness. You murdered Jeff. You murdered the eyewitness."

Martel's eyes widened. "Then what's stopping us from murdering you?"

Zelda rolled her eyes. "For goddess' sake, how many bodies have you gotten rid of on this island?"

The question was rhetorical, but Keawe stared up at the ceiling and held up fingers one by one like he was counting. Martel's lips turned up in a smile. "Just this island? Probably about as many as you've slept with."

Zelda moved, and I reached for her hand, thinking I could hold her back. Instead, she shifted her weight and squeezed my hand before she pushed it away. "Do you leave them all in the lava fields like you did Shane?"

Martel shook his head. "That was a special one just for you. It's what we planned to do to you once we get the artifact."

I exhaled. "You did kill Shane and stage the murder scene in the lava fields?"

He nodded. "The boy had outlived his usefulness."

"And he was asking for a cut of *our* profits." Keawe cursed and shook his head. "Can you believe that? All the work we did, and that little shit wanted more."

Martel patted Keawe's bouncing leg. "We were hoping to scare the hell out of both of you, but it didn't work. You two have to be some crazy women to not be scared right now."

My chin lifted. "Like your mama and aunties?" I remembered what Sam had said about Martel's female relatives.

His face reddened, and his cheeks began to shake. "Don't bring my mother into this."

Zelda cleared her throat. "You meant to scare us, and it didn't work. Seems like you two use the island and its culture for your own benefit."

"The island has many ways of getting rid of things you don't want found," Keawe said. "But for you two, I think the ocean will be a good resting place."

How the hell did I think we could outsmart these two killers? I had gotten us in over our heads, and it would cost us our lives.

Zelda shifted in her seat again. "It doesn't matter what we say or do, you're going to take the artifact and kill us. Do I have that right?" Her voice held no trace of fear.

Martel chuckled under his breath. "Finally, the woman gets it." He slapped his thighs and stood. "Now, either you show us where it is, or we'll rip you both apart and then kill you."

Zelda nodded. "Fantastic."

Keawe stood and rested his hands on his hips when his radio squeaked to life. *110 to 101, a bunch of Feds are swarming through the lobby. Over.*

Keawe and Martel exchanged a glance. Martel's hand reached for his holster. Zelda pulled an object from beneath the seat cushion and pointed it at Martel. It resembled a scanner I used to dispense medications at the hospital. But that little gizmo never shot things out the end of it. They hit Martel in the gut; he fell, contorted in pain.

Keawe took one hard stare at Martel on the floor and ran. He made it through the door and into the hall before shouts of "FBI!" filled the air.

Koa flew into the room just as Zelda dropped the thing in her hand. "Lex." He stepped over Martel's withering body, pulled me from the couch, and wrapped me in his arms. "If anything had happened to you—"

Breathing in his scent, I relaxed into his arms. "You heard everything?"

He pulled back and sighed. "Yeah, they got it all. Martel and Keawe will be going away for a long time." He glanced at Martel, now curled into a fetal position and unmoving on the floor. "Zelda, honey, how long did you use the stun gun?"

"Long enough for him not to get back up?" She kicked Martel's foot and got no response. "Oh shit, did I actually kill someone?"

I pushed Koa aside and knelt beside Martel to feel for a pulse. It was rapid and thready—not unheard of after a hit from a stun gun. "Doesn't look like you killed him." I glanced up at Koa. "We'll need medical support in here to be safe." He nodded and left the condo.

Zelda barely kicked Martel's foot again. "You know, Lexi, I was sad when you were mostly dead. This guy…I'm kinda sorry he's not totally dead."

I couldn't help but smile. Zelda and I could take on anything together. "Lucky for you he's not, or you would be experiencing a prison for real."

Emergency medical personnel hurried into the room. We stepped aside. A paramedic approached us and we held up our hands. "No, no, we're fine. Him," we said and pointed at Martel, who had begun moaning.

Zelda and I moved towards the door. I leaned into

the hall to take in the commotion. A few guests' doors were open with a few heads poking out to inspect the commotion. Two women in black outfits with thick vests that had large letters reading "FBI" had Keawe pushed against the wall, his wrists cuffed and behind his back.

"You two." His words were like venom. "We should have gotten rid of you when we had the chance. You're nothing but trouble."

Zelda and I choked out nervous laughs. Too many emotions in too short a time flowed through us and needed release. She stepped close to him. "First rule of dealing with middle-aged women: always assume we're trouble. Second rule: never underestimate our intelligence or pettiness."

The agents pulled Keawe off the wall. "Looks like he did all that and then some," one said as she dragged him down the hall.

The medical team worked fast and had Martel on a stretcher and out of the condo in no time. Koa stood at the end of the hall in animated conversation with another law enforcement officer. They shook hands, and Koa headed our way.

Zelda grabbed me by the arm and dragged me into the condo. "Lexi, do not mess this up," she whispered. "You're free, and Stache is available. Lock it down."

Koa appeared in the doorway behind Zelda.

"Zel…"

She shook her black curls. "No, you listen to me. That man is into you, and you like him. You know it. I know it. Hell, the whole island knows it." She dropped her hands to her side in exasperation. I glanced behind her to him, whose mouth was now turned up in a smile. "We're not getting any younger, and if a man looked at me the way he looks at you, girl—" Her voice pleaded with me to understand her.

Koa held up a finger to his lips in a quiet gesture. He moved behind Zelda and rested his hands on her shoulders, his mouth inches from her ear. "Thanks for your vote."

The words were barely out of his mouth when Zelda screamed, spun around, and pummeled him. Fists and curls, and possibly feet, flew as she laid into him. He laughed and attempted to dodge her blows until agents appeared and subdued her.

"It's fine, guys. Let her go," he said, out of breath. "I deserved that." They released her and she adjusted her t-shirt.

"Rule number three: Don't surprise a middle-aged woman. Ever."

Koa still gasped for breath. "Understood." He stood and stretched. "Ladies, how about I take you out to a nice dinner? My treat?"

Butterflies circled in my stomach anew. "It's the least you can do after that." Zelda dropped on the couch. "Maybe tomorrow? It's too late, and all I want is my bed."

I locked eyes with Koa, heat rose in my cheeks. "Same."

Chapter Twenty-Three

Zelda sighed loudly and turned to me. "Can life get any better?"

I shook my head and surveyed as the waves crashed onto Ashley Cregg's private beach. Zelda and I had found it impossible to stay at the resort once everything calmed down. Too many curious tourists stared and gossiped any time we left the room. Cregg graciously invited us to stay at his guest house, which was still bigger than both of our houses back home. And even better, my parents stayed in the main house. They were far enough away we could relax without their chatter but still enjoy their company.

As I stared, Koa broke through the waves and sauntered through the surf towards us. A huge smile broke out across my face. "Nope, I can't think of how it could get any better."

Zelda scooted her sunglasses down her nose. "Okay, yeah...your life is pretty great." She leaned forward. "Koa, you got a brother?" she yelled.

He picked up a towel and dried off. "Not one that I don't like."

Zelda roared with laughter. They had fallen into an easy friendship and teased each other like siblings. It was rare that Zelda and my paramour were friendly.

"Aren't you an only child?" I asked. Since the arrest of Martel and Keawe, Koa and I had the opportunity to spend more time alone. Some of it talking and sharing more about each other. A lot of it involved not talking.

He stretched out on the lounger next to me. "You remembered."

I shrugged. "I'm good at some things."

"I know you are," he said with a wink. My heart melted, and the warmth that spread through my body had nothing to do with the sun.

A towel struck me across the body. "Cool it, both of you." Zelda used her best teacher's voice but didn't bother to hide the smile in her gaze.

Properly chastised, I couldn't wipe the smile from my face. I leaned back and closed my eyes. The breeze ruffled my hair and dried the ocean water from my skin.

Koa's phone dinged. He squinted at the screen. "Zelda, you are officially in the clear." He waved the phone in the air. "Sam just got the word. He'll bring by the documents this evening."

"Yay!" She did a cheer with her arms. "Now I can finally relax."

I gave her an eye. "Like that's not what got you into this situation to begin with."

She blew a raspberry in my direction.

Koa continued. "What it means is now you can officially leave the island."

His words sat heavy on me. If we were free to leave, that meant we could return to our lives in the Midwest. And that also meant leaving Hawaii and Koa behind. I had denied my feelings for him for too long, and now that I had given into him and those feelings, I wasn't sure I was ready to give it up. And if I was completely honest with myself, I didn't want to.

"You know, I'm going to go tell your parents."

Zelda pushed herself up from the lounger with a grunt and groan. "I'll see you at lunch?"

"Yep." I waved as she strolled across the sand to the lawn and the main house.

Silence fell again between us. Koa focused on his phone, and I fumbled with my e-reader. He sighed and dropped his phone in his beach bag. "You'll be going home soon." It was a statement, not a question. Like he knew the answer already.

I closed the e-reader and stared at the horizon, unable to meet his gaze. Not trusting my voice, I nodded.

"I don't want you to go. Stay. The hospital needs nurses. You can make a life here."

The lump in my throat grew and threatened to cut off my oxygen. This was a world away from my life back home, from real life. And a world away from Zelda.

He reached for my hand and squeezed it. "Lexi, honey. Say something."

I coughed uncontrollably and needed to go to the bathroom. I waved and held up a single finger before I stumbled into the house. A quick trip and a splash of water on my face calmed me down. I soothed down my uncontrollable, frizzy hair and headed back outside to face my future.

I settled comfortably into the lounger. One thing about Ashley Cregg, he enjoyed comfort, and I appreciated that. "Koa, I...I'm not ready to leave Atherton quite yet."

He turned to face me and propped himself up on an elbow. "I thought you'd say that."

His tone broke my heart. "I'm sorry. I wish I felt different. My life is back there."

He reached for my hand and held it lightly. "Could

you ever see your life here? With me?"

I made a guttural noise and regretted it. "With you? Absolutely. Here?" I shook my head. "This isn't real life. It is, I know, but it's not. Does that make sense?"

He dropped my hand; the action set me adrift. "It does. I felt like that when I moved back. It took an adjustment, but I made it. So will you."

All the possible arguments for and against this relationship ran through my head. Zelda could visit. My parents would visit. Clearly, since they enjoy spending time with Cregg so much. But it wasn't the same. It wouldn't be the same. It would be a whole new life, and I wasn't sure at my age I could pick up everything and move to paradise.

He sat up and faced me. "Lexi, I love you. You are the balm to my soul. We are smart adults, and if we're both committed to this, we can make it work."

I nodded and swallowed hard. "I'm not ready for this to end, but I need time to think. And now that we can leave, I don't know how to feel." I faced him. "Or what to do. I want to try."

His face lit up, and he kissed me. His lips tasted of salt and the sun. Even so, I felt like a cloud passed in front of the sun.

With our departure imminent, there were things I needed to take care of. Sure, Zelda was cleared of all crime and Martel and Keawe would be going away for a long time. But as I stared at the underwear drawer and the artifact tucked between my granny panties, I realized this was one thing I must do.

Lifting it out of the drawer, the sun caught it, and I was in awe of the beauty of it. It was possible this was otherworldly and a gift from the gods altogether. I made no pretenses with a cover for it or hide it but held it firm in my hand as I marched out of the guesthouse, headed toward the main house.

I nodded to Vanna and other staff as I entered the main house. Even with all the amazing artwork and design, it was beginning to feel like a home. I could see why Cregg loved this place so much. I found him in the library. Glasses perched on the end of his nose, he leaned back in a leather chair with a book in his lap that looked to weigh more than him.

He glanced up when I knocked softly on the dark, shiny wood. "Lexi, come on in." He lifted the book off his lap and sat it on the table next to him. "I didn't see you at lunch."

I shook my head and took the seat across from him. The cool, smooth leather engulfed me. "No, I...since Zelda is cleared, I needed to make plans to return to Atherton."

His brow furrowed. "Needed, not wanted." He let the words hang in the air.

I didn't respond. I was here for one thing and needed to get it done. The artifact remained in my hand, and I held it out to him. "I thought after all of this, you might want this?"

Cregg stared at the artifact as the sun danced off it for a long time before his brows rose. "No. No, I don't want it. I don't want to touch it."

I sputtered words. "But if there's any truth to the myth behind it, even a little, what harm will it do?"

He uncrossed his legs and leaned forward. "Alexandra, if I may call you that?" I nodded. "I've lived a long life. A good one. I've done some bad things, and I've made some mistakes, but I've done it all with the best of intentions." With a sigh, he rested his elbows on his thighs. "I'll tell you a secret. There is no curse, no chance for eternal life. There is just this one, and we must make it count."

I couldn't tear my gaze from his. He was speaking about his life, but it seemed to me his words were meant for me. "But what if..."

He reached out and grasped my free hand. "Stop with the what ifs and maybes and all of it. Follow your damn heart, Alexandria. Do it now. Don't go to your grave with the regrets I have." My finger bones cracked under his steel grip. I nodded and tore my hand from his with effort. "I've commissioned a replica of the artifact to be placed on display in the museum in case anyone else gets the same ideas. This will go into the vaults of the museum for safekeeping."

I stared down at the object in my hand. Everything Cregg said made sense, but I had to want to believe in not only myself, but also to trust in the crazy idea that everything would work out as it was meant to. That I could be in a relationship with someone on the other side of the planet, and it would somehow work out. I could still have my best friend be the same as ever and not lose a thing. If it had been Zelda in this situation, she would have already moved in and redecorated Koa's house. I envied her for trusting things would work out.

"I'm afraid of losing..." The whispered words hung between us.

Cregg leaned back in the chair with a sigh. "Oh, my dear, that is the real curse." I nodded and tore my gaze from his. "If you would, leave that on the desk. I'll have the curator come by this afternoon." With a sniffle, I laid the artifact that had caused so much trouble on the desk and walked away.

The stone path to the guesthouse seemed short, and I stopped on an outcrop of black rock. Waves crashed around me, and drops of ocean spray sprinkled onto me. I sat with my knees bent up and stared out at the waves. I had a decision to make, and knew the only way I would be able to make it would be with my best friend's okay.

Chapter Twenty-Four

The celebration of Zelda's official freedom was to be that evening at the main house. We donned our nice breezy dresses and headed down the stone path to the house. Tiki torches lit the night, giving the evening a mythical atmosphere. I sighed heavily, and Zelda stopped on the stone path. "What's wrong?"

I stopped and huffed. "Koa wants me to stay." The words hung in the night like the smoke from the torches. She shrugged and started down the path again. I hurried after her. "Wait, did you hear what I said?"

She slowed. "I heard you." She stopped and threw her hands on her hips. "I feel like we've had this conversation more than a few times now. I'm not going to rehash it for the one thousandth time. Crap, I'd rather throw one of these rocks at your head and knock some sense into you than go over this again."

"But it would mean we would be so far away from each other," I said, my voice small. That was one thing we hadn't discussed. Zelda and I hadn't spent our entire lives together, but it seemed like the older we got, the closer we got, if that was possible. And I couldn't imagine a world where we couldn't simply go see each other whenever we wanted, and it not cost a small fortune.

She threw her hair back and stared into the night sky. When she lowered her face, her eyes were wet. "I don't want to lose you, and I won't lose you. You mean the world to me. But your happiness is equally important. If we've learned anything on this trip, it's that life is too short for stupid shit." She let out a dry laugh. "And we've done a lot of stupid shit over the years." I returned her smile. "You have the chance at real happiness...maybe take it?"

My heart threatened to jump out of my chest and tears flowed down my face.

Zelda tufted. "Now we're going to mess up our makeup." She wiped a finger expertly under an eye and made an unladylike snort.

I wrapped an arm around her, and we continued. "We can make it work. I wasn't going to give you up for a man."

"Oh, hell no. Sisters before Misters, one thousand percent. We've been through too much to leave each other." She squeezed me in a hug. "Plus, I look super cute in a swimsuit, and I want to learn to surf. Maybe pick up one of those sexy instructors in the process." She wiggled her eyebrows.

A sensation flowed through me. I wasn't sure what it was. Could it be contentment? I had my best friend, a great man. My parents were healthy and happy, and so was I.

Cregg had gone all out with the decorations at the main house. Tropical flowers covered every surface, and enough tiki torches lit the area to be seen from space.

Sam's crisp white shirt reflected the firelight as he stood with his arm around a woman who I could only describe as radiant. Zelda held out her arms to him, and they exchanged a long hug that ended with sniffs that covered tears on both sides.

"Marie, meet the girls." Sam returned his arm to the woman's shoulders. "Zelda, Lexi, meet my Marie."

"So happy to meet you ladies. I've heard so much about both of you," she said with a wink.

Zelda patted Marie on the shoulder. "And every word of it is true." She returned the wink.

"Girls, come here." Dad waved us over with a frothy cocktail in his hand.

Mom wore a muumuu so garish that even in the light of the tiki torches hurt my eyes. Dad wore a shirt to match.

Hugs were exchanged and drinks thrust into our hands. Cregg's usual pale countenance was brightened by an equally loud shirt. Zelda and I looked out of place in solid-colored dresses.

Cregg cleared his throat and held up his glass. "If I may have your attention. Friends. We are joined here tonight to celebrate the freedom of our dear Zelda." Whoops and cheers filled the night. He waited until the silence descended again and smiled at her. "Until she finds trouble again." Groans and nods as Zelda held up her hands in an innocent gesture. "Thank you all for bringing joy and friendship into my life in this season." His voice was serious. "And here's to new seasons and continued friendships." He raised his glass, and we toasted.

Dad yelled, "*L'chaim,*" so loud I feared loss of hearing in one ear. Food came off the grill and drinks flowed. Against the house, lit by the flames, Koa stood in a crisp white shirt.

My heart jumped out of my chest. Our eyes locked and I made straight for him. The whole way I had to remind myself to breathe. I stood in front of him as a small smile played at the corner of his lips.

"Good evening." His warm voice sent a shiver down my spine, like the first time I heard it that morning on the tour, except now I knew it was for all the right reasons. The attraction was real. It was mutual. And there was something deeper there, too, that sent shivers down my spine.

"Hey there." Embarrassed by the high pitch of my voice, I cleared my throat. "You look handsome."

He leaned down and grazed a kiss on my cheek. My body lit on fire. "You are gorgeous." I shimmied a shiver away and resisted the urge to do a little bounce when he chuckled. Would this sensation ever go away? I sure hoped not.

I cleared my throat. My hands ran down the sides of the drink glass. "I…I've…yes."

"Yes?" Koa questioned.

"I don't know how any of this is going to work, and I can't move here just yet. I'm not ready, but I love you, and…yes." I lifted my gaze to meet his and everything in his face said I made the right decision. I threw an arm around him. "I love you."

His lips found mine and, whatever happens, wherever we go, it'll be worth it.

With our arms wrapped around each other, we joined the rest of the group. Zelda and my eyes locked, and she raised her glass in a salute.

This was paradise.

A word about the author...

Emily Karmazin, a long-time fan of snacks and 80's television, currently lives in the Wasatch Mountains of Utah with her husband and their dogs. She wrote her first book in third grade, a fanfic of Little House on the Prairie. She has an interest in travel, reading, learning new things, hiking, all things strange and usual, and baking.

Follow her at www.emilykwriter.com or on social media for all the latest.